THE SCHOOL REUNION

ALSO BY SHALINI BOLAND

The Silent Bride
The Daughter-in-Law
A Perfect Stranger
The Family Holiday
The Couple Upstairs
My Little Girl
The Wife
One Of Us Is Lying
The Other Daughter
The Marriage Betrayal
The Girl From The Sea
The Best Friend
The Perfect Family
The Silent Sister
The Millionaire's Wife
The Child Next Door
The Secret Mother
Marchwood Vampire Series
Outside Series

THE SCHOOL REUNION

SHALINI BOLAND

This is a work of fiction. Names, characters, organizations, places, events, and incidents are either products of the author's imagination or are used fictitiously. Any resemblance to actual persons, living or dead, or actual events is purely coincidental.

Published by Thomas and Mercer, Seattle

www.apub.com

ISBN-13: 9781662507090
eISBN: 9781662507106

Cover design by Faceout Studio, Spencer Fuller
Cover image: © BlueSkyImage © Casper1774 Studio / Shutterstock

Printed in the United States of America

To all those who managed to get through their school days in one piece. And to all those who didn't.

Prologue

Icy rain slashes your face, making you blink and gasp as you clutch the knife, holding it out in front of you so that it's clearly visible. Its serrated blade beads with dark raindrops that look like blood.

You step forward, blocking out distractions – the distant thud of music and laughter that's trying to pull you back to sanity, the scent of distant snow and rotting bonfires that burns your nostrils. All this normality trying to turn you away. Instead, you take another step, pushing your hatred ahead of you so that it's quite obvious what you intend to do here tonight. That you mean business.

Despite the painful pounding of your heart and the sharpness in your lungs, you're ready for this. You've already watched numerous videos online and read up about the different stabbing techniques. You practised holding this very knife in the kitchen, making sure that your grip was firm. That you knew what you were doing so that you wouldn't fumble or drop it. So that everything would be perfect.

But that was back when you were alone and calm inside a warm, dry house. Not out here shivering, riled up with alcohol and fury, with sweating palms and trembling fingers. Facing the person who destroyed your life.

Chapter One

CHLOE

I shift in my chair, trying to concentrate on my emails, but the sun blazes through the windows, making it hard to see my laptop screen, and Mum won't stop jabbering in my ear.

'I'm just saying, you could have got more out of him, Chloe,' she continues, gazing critically at one of my sofas before leaning down and gathering up the various scatter cushions. 'He was very tight-fisted towards you in the settlement. You should've got yourself a better solicitor.'

'Mum, you don't have to do that. Sit down and relax.'

'No, it's fine. You know I enjoy it. They had their cushions arranged like this in Marks & Spencer. Trust me, Chloe, you'll love it when I'm done.' She plumps up my favourite velvet cushion, puts it back a few inches to the left and karate-chops the top of it.

I pull one of the curtains across, blocking out the sun's rays, and return to the dining table. That's better, now I can see what's on the screen. I frown at an email that's just come through with the subject heading 'West Cliff School Reunion'. Just seeing the name of my old school makes me feel quite wobbly. I click on it and start skim-reading.

'Anywa-ay, as I was saying,' Mum continues, 'you let Ben get away with far too much in the divorce. He could've afforded to treat you right after all the years you've been together. If you'd pushed, you could've had a nice big house and enough money in the bank for the rest of your life. I don't know why you let him take advantage. You're too much of a soft touch.'

Mum's rant distracts me from the email for a moment. 'I'm fine. More than fine. Anyway, I love my flat.' I glance around the beautiful living room with its tall sash windows, a trademark of these Georgian apartments on the Royal Crescent. I still can't believe I live here. That I own a slice of Bath's history. The eighteenth-century row of houses curves around a huge lawn, which means I have a wonderful view from the living room and from my bedroom. The building is more like something you'd see in Versailles than in North Somerset. It was one of my ex-husband's rental properties, but he gave it to me in the divorce settlement eighteen months ago. I wasn't able to move in until a year later, when the tenant finally moved out. It's been a long, stressful road, but I'm gradually feeling . . . if not exactly happy, at least more settled.

'Financial security's hard to come by.' My mother straightens up and turns to face me, her blonde highlights harsh against her powdered skin and patchy pink lipstick. 'I should know. I've been struggling for years.'

'I know, Mum,' I reply with a sigh. My parents never married, and my dad left us when I was a baby. Not long after that, he started a new life with a new family. Mum won't talk about him, or them, and I've stopped asking. I've accepted that he'll never be part of my life and that's fine by me.

My mother's faded blue eyes cloud with tears but she sniffs them away. 'And now your Ben's living in a huge country house with a new wife and two beautiful babies. That could've been you . . . if you'd managed to keep hold of him.' She mutters that last bit under her breath.

I inhale and try to think calming thoughts as she continues with her never-ending tirade. She's been staying with me for a long weekend – and boy has it been long. All she's talked about has been my failed marriage and – as she sees it – failed life. 'It didn't work out, Mum. I'm not going to be stuck in a relationship that isn't right. No matter how much money he's got, or how big his house is.'

'Yes, but you still haven't explained what made him leave, Chloe. Not really. Not properly. Was there something he wasn't getting from you? I know it's not very PC of me to say it, but men need to feel like they're the centre of your world, not an afterthought.'

'Mum! This isn't the 1950s. Haven't you heard of equal rights?'

'Yes, yes, okay, okay.' She tuts. 'But you do have a tendency to be quite selfish.'

'Thanks a lot!'

'No point getting offended. If I can't say it, Chloe, then who can? It's like body odour, isn't it. Only a mother can point it out.'

I stifle a laugh, even though I feel like throttling her just to shut her up for a minute.

'It's not a laughing matter, Chloe. Men need to be treated with care and attention.' She shakes her head. 'Like cats. If you don't give them a gentle stroke and a bowl of food every so often, they start looking elsewhere.'

'Mum!' There's no point trying to change my mother's mind on this. She's so terrified about me being on my own, like her, that she'd rather I lived an unhappy life with a man than a contented one alone. It's not as though I wouldn't *like* to be in a relationship – of course I would – but Ben was an entitled arsehole. His new wife, the wonderful Wendi, is welcome to him.

'Be honest: did he cheat on you, Chloe?' Mum asks for the hundredth time, her eyes narrowing. 'I wish you'd tell me what really happened instead of pretending everything's fine.'

'I already said he didn't.' I flush, looking down at my laptop. I'm not about to tell my mother the truth. She'd never let it drop.

'Ta-da!' Mum announces, coming to stand by my side at the dining table as she regards her handiwork. 'And I've draped the throw I got you for your birthday over the arm of the sofa.'

'That's lovely, Mum,' I gush. 'Looks really stylish.' Although, to be quite honest, I can't see much of a difference.

'Do you think so?' Mum's tone brightens. 'I always thought I should have gone into interior design. But we didn't get the same opportunities back in my day. Not like you lot with your careers advice and fancy school.' She scowls and shakes her head. 'Not that you made the most of your school days, Chloe. Too busy chasing the wrong sort of boys . . .'

I tune her out, and decide to delete the West Cliff email without reading the rest. I wish they'd never sent it. I should have changed my email address after leaving school. Going to the reunion would be a bad idea. West Cliff is the private school I attended back home in Bournemouth, where I grew up. I was lucky enough to win a full swimming scholarship at the age of eleven. But that acceptance letter didn't turn out to be the blessing it appeared to be. To this day, the smell of chlorine triggers bad memories.

'What's that?' Mum asks, making me jump. I realise she's hovering at my shoulder, peering at the screen in front of me.

'Nothing.' I snap my laptop shut. 'What do you fancy eating tonight?'

'A reunion?' Mum's voice perks up. 'When is it?'

'Not sure, but it doesn't matter, because I'm not going.' My heart has started thumping. The last thing I need is to start dwelling on the past. The present is hard enough.

'*Not going?* Why on earth not?' Mum plonks herself down adjacent to me at the dining table.

'Because—'

'Because, from where I'm sitting,' she steamrollers on, 'you're a thirty-one-year-old divorcee with no boyfriend, no social life and – let's face it, Chloe, love – a boring job.'

The air leaves my lungs with a soft whoosh.

Mum purses her lips and raises an overplucked eyebrow, daring me to contradict her.

'Jeez, Mum, tell it like it is, why don't you? And, anyway, my job isn't *that* boring,' I protest half-heartedly.

'You work in a bank where everyone is almost twice your age and is either happily married or a grandparent.' Mum parrots an earlier conversation back at me. I knew I shouldn't have confided in her; knew she'd wheel out my frustrations to use against me. 'You need to put yourself out there, Chloe. Say yes to all the invitations you get. Life is passing you by. If I was your age again . . .' She shakes her head. I know Mum resents the fact that I went to a private school. She's always telling me how she would have loved to have had the advantages I did. How I'd squandered my talent and wasted my opportunities.

'Do you want a coffee?' I get to my feet, needing to put some physical space between us, even if it's only as far as the kitchen.

'You need to go to that reunion, Chloe,' Mum pushes. 'It'll be good for you. I wish I'd been invited to a school reunion. I'd have accepted like a shot. Although most of my classmates were boring as sin.' She follows me into the tiny galley kitchen next to the living room. The size of this room is the only downside to the flat as I absolutely adore cooking and would've enjoyed a bit more space. But, as the building is Grade I listed, I doubt I'll be able to knock down any walls. It's a small price to pay to live here, though.

'Do you want some of my apple cake with your coffee?' I ask, hoping to distract her.

'I shouldn't . . .' She puts a hand to her trim stomach. 'But go on then. I must've put on a stone since I got here.'

'You look great, Mum.'

She glances around the cramped kitchen and sniffs. 'Anyway, stop trying to change the subject. This reunion – will Chris be there?'

I give an internal shudder as I remember my first boyfriend, Chris Tamber. He was the boy everyone wanted to know, to be, or to be noticed by. For some unknown reason, he eventually chose me. But being Chris Tamber's girlfriend wasn't all it was cracked up to be.

'Put half a teaspoon of sugar in my coffee, love, I feel like I have low blood sugar.' She presses a hand to her forehead.

I do as she asks.

'So,' she persists, trying to catch my eye. '*Chris* – will he be there? I heard he's recently separated from his wife. You could do worse than land a man like Chris. One of the richest men in the county, I heard.'

'It's not all about money, Mum.'

'Tell me that when you're sixty and can't pay the bills.'

'You can pay your bills, can't you, Mum?' I suddenly worry that maybe she's in financial difficulty. Mum works as a manager at Tesco Express. She loves her job, even though she moans about it all the time.

'Me?' She snorts. 'I've got my head screwed on, Chloe. I might never be able to retire, mind you. Be working till I drop dead. No, it's you I'm worried about. You may have a fancy flat right now, but the maintenance charges for a place like this must be the price of a small mortgage. You need to plan for your future.'

'I will, Mum. But I'll do it on my own. I don't need Ben or Chris or any other rich dickhead to boss me around.'

'But—'

'And, before you say anything else, I'm absolutely *not* going to that reunion.'

Mum clamps her jaw shut and scowls.

I turn away to reach for the Dorset apple cake, take a knife from the block and savagely slice into the soft sponge, trying to push out all thoughts of West Cliff School. Fighting against those dark memories that are suddenly threatening to escape the carefully sealed box in my mind.

Chapter Two

DEAN

'Did you live here when you were little?' Ellis asks, his blue eyes wide with interest, his lashes so long they sweep his cheeks when he blinks.

'I did,' I reply, crouching to his level and tweaking his nose.

He laughs and pushes my hand away. 'Daddy!'

'What? Why can't I have your nose? I just want to borrow it.'

'No, it's mine,' Ellis giggles.

'What about a swap? You can have my nose . . .' I mime trying to remove my nose. 'No, it's really stuck on there.'

Ellis holds his stomach as he belly-laughs. 'Daddy, you're so silly.'

I might be laughing and joking with my five-year-old son, but on the inside I feel sad enough to sleep for a hundred years. Ellis is the one good thing in my life right now. Everything else has gone to shit.

Today, we're here packing away Mum's clothes. I've been putting off doing this for weeks, but last night I had a dream where she and I were baking a cake, and today I woke up feeling like I had to just get on and sort things out. She died three months ago, after a quick and vicious bout of cancer. I barely had time to process her illness before she was gone. It still feels unreal. And although I'm a thirty-three-year-old man, I feel like a lost child. An orphan.

Ellis pulls one of Mum's dresses over his head – a sparkly green number – and twirls around the room in it. The hem drags on the ground. I remember Mum wearing it one evening when she and my stepdad went to a friend's birthday party. She worried it was too flashy.

Being in our family home without her here feels so wrong. I don't understand how I'm now the person in charge. The grown-up. While she was alive, I felt like I was the one looking after her – taking her out, sorting out problems with the house, with the bills. But now I realise that my big-man act was an illusion. She was the one who was there for *me*. My emotional rock, which – I'm beginning to realise – meant way more than all the other peripheral stuff.

Since the age of eighteen, it's been me and Mum against the world. My younger sister died when she was sixteen, and my stepdad died from a heart attack six months later. It was a brutal time. But Mum and I got through it together, moment by painful moment.

'I thought you were supposed to be helping me, Ellis.' I stand and watch him as he heaps on his grandmother's necklaces and bracelets, jangling them around.

'I am helping. I'm making you happy with my dances,' he replies, executing a pirouette, his hands pointed above his head.

I pick him up and hold him close, the faint scent of Mum's perfume making me shut my eyes against the emotions threatening to overwhelm me.

He gives me a sloppy kiss on my cheek and wriggles to be let down.

'Right,' I say, taking a deep breath and setting him back on the carpet. 'Let's make a plan. You can pass me the clothes from those drawers, and I'll fold them up and put them into the bags for the charity shop, okay?'

'Okay, Daddy.' He opens the bottom drawer and passes me an armful of socks while singing loudly.

I stare at the socks in my arms, wondering if I can give second-hand socks to charity. Or is that gross? They're clean, and in good condition. I don't know. I'll just put them in the bag, and think about it later. The doorbell interrupts my thoughts. I've no idea who it could be. Hopefully not someone who doesn't know about Mum. It's been horrible having to tell people. Seeing the shock and confusion on their faces. Having to comfort them while trying to keep it together myself.

'Let's see who that is.' I take Ellis's hand and we walk down the beige-carpeted stairs to the wide tiled hallway. I take a steadying breath and open the door.

It's Mum's next-door neighbour, Mrs Parsons. She's holding a flowery metal tin in her hand and has a kind smile on her face. 'Dean, how are you? I saw you were here and brought some home-made biscuits round – chocolate chip. I thought Ellis might like them. Well, both of you, actually.'

'Thank you. What do you say, Ellis?' I prompt.

'Thank you, Mrs Parsons.'

'You're very welcome,' she replies, her brown eyes crinkling. 'And I must say you do look very sparkly today, Ellis.'

'It's Granny's dress,' he explains.

'Thanks for these, Mrs Parsons,' I add. 'That's really so kind of you.'

'I think it's time you called me Marilyn,' she says to me.

Marilyn Parsons has lived next door since before my parents bought the place. I've known her all my life. She used to teach at my primary school, but now she's retired and sadly widowed. She and her husband were good friends with my parents.

'Come in,' I offer. 'I think we have tea. Not sure about milk though.'

She follows me through to the kitchen, where she busies herself with the tea things and puts a few of her biscuits on to a willow-pattern plate. Then she nips next door to fetch a pint of milk.

'We're tackling Mum's wardrobe,' I explain when she returns.

She pats the back of my hand. 'You're a good boy. I'm sorry about your mum. She was a lovely lady. One of my best friends.' She presses her lips together and swallows.

'Thanks, I know. You must miss her too.'

'I do. Very much.'

I open the back door to let in some air, and we sit at the round pine table, sipping our tea and listening to Ellis loudly crunching his biscuit while he hums a tune and rhythmically kicks the table leg.

'I suppose you'll put this place on the market now,' Marilyn says carefully, putting her mug down.

I realise she must be worried about who might move in next. 'Actually, I was thinking that Ellis and I might move in here.'

'Oh, that would be lovely!' Mrs Parsons claps her hands, her face lighting up.

My son looks across at me, and asks through a mouthful of biscuit, 'Is this going to be our house now, Daddy?'

'Maybe,' I reply cagily. I'd planned to tell Ellis at a later date, not wanting him to worry about moving, but it seems I've let the cat out of the bag.

My son and I currently live together in my two-bedroom flat, not too far from here. It's nice, but cramped, and there's no outside space at all. I'm also very aware of the neighbours on the floor below, who are always complaining that Ellis is too noisy. He's not noisy. He's just a normal five-year-old. So, after Mum died, I decided that it might be great to move in here and rent out the flat to cover the mortgage. That is, if I'm not forced to sell them both. I feel sick at the thought of the mess I'm in, but I try to push those worries aside for the moment.

Mum's house is in a lovely part of Westbourne, close to the beach and the shops. This area never used to be as desirable, and we always thought of our house as just a regular kind of home in a regular kind of road. But over the last couple of decades, prices have shot up. The house has three bedrooms and a decent-sized garden. It needs a lot of work to modernise it but, as a building contractor, I could do most of it myself. Once it's been refurbished, I can then make the decision whether we keep it for ourselves or sell up and buy somewhere smaller. But I can't do anything until it's gone through probate, which could take months.

'I haven't definitely decided,' I reply.

'No, of course not.' Marilyn nods. 'But surely it's the perfect family home for the two of you? And if you were next door, I'd be more than happy to mind Ellis whenever you needed.'

'Wow, that's very generous of you, Mrs Par— Marilyn.' As a single dad, I can't deny that having a trusted babysitter living next door would be very convenient during the school holidays.

'Not at all. It would be my pleasure. Ellis and I are great friends, aren't we?' The two of them share a smile.

Ellis nods. 'Me and Granny and Mrs Parsons like to talk about things. And we like biscuits and doing the garden.'

'Well, that all sounds very enjoyable,' I reply, giving my son's shoulders a squeeze.

We spend the next twenty minutes chatting about Mum and reminiscing about my primary school days back when Marilyn used to teach me. Ellis is fascinated by the idea of me as a five-year-old.

'Wait here a minute,' Marilyn says, getting to her feet. She leaves the kitchen and returns with a photo album, showing Ellis a picture of me and my sister when we were little. The sight of it makes my vision blur. I still can't believe my sister's gone.

'Hope you don't mind me getting this album out,' Marilyn says. 'Sorry, I'm forgetting it's your house now. Your mum and I used to treat each other's homes like our own. I'll stop doing that.' She reddens, realising she may have overstepped the mark.

'It's fine, I don't mind,' I reply. If Marilyn's going to be looking after Ellis from time to time, then I want her to feel comfortable here.

'Well, I'd better be going,' she says. 'Let you two get on with your day. Thank you for the tea. And I do hope you will decide to move in. Your mum and dad would have loved the thought of you two making the place your own.'

I nod, balling my fists against another wall of emotion.

She turns away to give me a moment, and then Ellis and I see her to the door.

'They were nice biscuits!' my son calls after her.

She waves and closes the gate, making her way back to her house along the dusty pavement.

I ruffle Ellis's fair hair that's so like mine – blond, thick and unruly – wondering if maybe this house has too many sad memories for us to consider moving back.

'Shall we do more of Granny's clothes?' Ellis asks, heading to the staircase.

I close the front door, feeling the weight of empty silence around us. My motivation to carry on clearing out Mum's room has completely vanished. It all suddenly feels too much. 'Maybe later,' I reply, turning around, knowing that I should just grit my teeth and do it now, because it's not something I want hanging over me.

'Are we going to live here with *Mummy*?' Ellis asks, his eyes wide. Hopeful. Unaware that him asking about his mother has set my hackles rising.

It always breaks my heart and fuels my rage to hear Ellis ask about my ex-wife. We were married for six years until she left me for a wealthy finance guy three years ago. They now have two kids of their own together. She barely sees our son, and it makes me so angry when I think about how, out of the blue, she left us, with no other explanation than she'd fallen in love with someone else. *Fine. But what about your son?* I now have sole custody of Ellis, who's just the sweetest boy. Despite his puzzlement and hurt over his mum, he still gives his heart willingly. Too willingly.

I crouch in front of my son and stroke his soft cheek. 'It's going to be you and me living here together, buddy. What do you think?'

'Not Mummy?' Ellis asks, his chin wobbling slightly.

His mother leaving, coupled with the fact that my biological father left my mum when I was a baby, has made me fiercely protective of Ellis. Maybe more than I would otherwise have been. I never really clicked with my stepdad, and have always felt the absence of my real father – who I never met – so I'm keenly aware of Ellis's lack of a mother. I don't want him feeling abandoned or unwanted in any way. I always try to show him how important he is to me. How special and loved.

'Just you and me,' I reply, tapping Ellis's nose and then my own. 'The two of us having fun and making our own rules. What do you think?'

Ellis frowns for a moment before breaking into a grin. 'Yeah! Our own rules!' He starts leaping around the hallway and my chest squeezes with love.

Ellis is the reason I'm not interested in finding a new partner. I'm scared to risk his heart again, especially after he recently lost his grandmother too. No. Right now, it's me and my child against the world. And that's just how I like it.

Chapter Three

CHLOE

I say goodbye to my work colleagues and leave the bank, trudging up Milsom Street, crossing over to the shady side. I'm already sweating by the time I turn into George Street, where the early-evening sun hits me square in the face. I hurry across the road and up the steps on to the raised pavement, squinting and shading my eyes with my hands, then pressing myself against the railings as an oblivious loved-up couple amble past, taking up the whole of the narrow space.

It's only just after 5 p.m. but the bars and pubs are already filling up with the after-work crowd, and I catch glimpses of laughing groups of twenty-somethings and couples, along with the occasional family having an early supper. It's a sociable city. Friendly. At least, I used to think so.

I moved to Bath eleven years ago to be with Ben. We met in my home town of Bournemouth, seventy miles away, while he was on a stag weekend with five of his best friends. I was lifeguarding on Alum Chine beach that summer, and his best friend, Joel – the groom – was chatting me up. As best man, Ben came over to remind Joel that he was getting married in a week's time. Joel shuffled off sheepishly, leaving me with Ben. The two of us hit it off. Ben said I looked hot in my lifeguard uniform of red shorts and yellow top – trust me, I didn't.

But the outcome of moving to Bath to be with him was that all Ben's friends became my friends. And then, when we divorced, I lost them all. Which can make living here pretty uncomfortable at times. I'm always bumping into people I used to socialise with. People who I thought had become lifelong friends. More fool me. A couple of them have even changed banks so there won't be any awkward encounters where I work, despite the fact that it's nearly all done online these days.

I considered moving back to Bournemouth after the divorce – I could probably have got a transfer to a different branch – but that would've felt like defeat. I've created a life here. I do have a few friends that I made in my own right, and a couple of friends from Ben's circle who are his friends' exes. But they're either married without much time to socialise, or they're not quite my type of people. I also have my beautiful apartment, and my job. I'm hoping, with time, that things will improve. But how much more time will it take?

I pass The Goat, one of our favourite pubs – the place we celebrated our engagement. Loss hits me square in the chest. It's lively in there tonight. Anna behind the bar catches my eye and gives me a wave. I give a half-smile, wondering if I should go in for a quick drink, but anxiety gets the better of me. She won't have time to chat, and then I'll just be drinking alone at the bar. I'd love to be one of those types of women who have the confidence to drink alone, eat out at a restaurant with nothing but a book for company, or do a solo holiday, but I'm not bold enough. Not yet anyway. Maybe it's something you have to work up to.

I'm now starting to regret walking past The Goat without popping in. Maybe I should go back and have that solo drink. Prove to myself that I can do it. I might even enjoy myself. But I'm already several hundred yards up the road now, and, besides, I'm in my frumpy work suit. I continue on, telling myself it's early days. Eighteen months is no time at all. Not for me, anyway. Ben though . . . he got right back in the saddle. Although our marriage started falling apart two years before we officially ended it.

I guess Ben didn't turn out to be the person I thought he was. He's become a stranger. Someone I can no longer rely on or trust. It's funny to think you know someone so well that you believe they'll stick by you through anything, and then . . . I give myself an internal shake. It's no good dwelling on the past like this, wondering *what if.* I need to focus on a future without him. I should cut myself some slack. Give myself more time to make new friends, a new life. Maybe I'll enrol in some kind of class, or retrain, go to college, go for that solo drink . . .

This cycle of thoughts has been a recurring theme over the past few months – I'll start to feel hopeless and sad about my life, then I'll convince myself that I'm going to do something to snap out of it. Only I never do. And now another Friday evening has rolled around and I have nothing more interesting planned than a chilled bottle of rosé, a Waitrose lasagne and a bagged salad. No night out with friends, no date. I'm starting to think I'll never meet anyone again. I stop walking for a moment and take a breath. Come on, Chloe, get a grip. I'm not normally so maudlin. I start moving again with a more determined stride.

Thoughts of the reunion trickle into my brain like water trying to get into a leaky boat. Question is, are these thoughts going to sink me? Or was my mum right? Should I have accepted the invitation? Or am I stupid to be even considering it? My stomach lurches at the thought of seeing all those familiar faces, at the thought of actually talking to my classmates after years of no contact.

If Ben and I were still together, I'd have had no qualms about deleting the email unopened. Which is daft, because surely the whole point of these things is to show everyone how wonderfully everything has turned out for you, with the perfect spouse, the perfect life. What would I be showing them now? That I'm divorced, in a dead-end job, with no friends. I shake my head. *No.* That I'm happily single, with a successful career in banking and my own stunning Grade-I listed apartment. I guess it's how you spin things, right?

My heart has started pounding uncomfortably. I realise I'm thinking about the reunion on a superficial level, without considering the deeper consequences of attending. I daren't peel back the outer layers to my thoughts. It's like I'm skating across the top of the ice, ignoring the darkness beneath my feet. But is it so wrong to want some happiness again? To put myself out there, despite the risk?

I reach the Circus roundabout, striding past the elegant curved facades of the Georgian townhouses with their columns, white-painted doors and smart black railings. I quicken my pace, suddenly keen to get home and retrieve the email from the deleted folder. To study the invitation and see exactly when and where the reunion is being held. Am I brave enough to accept it? To see those people again? We've all grown up now. Moved on. It could be a chance for some closure. Or maybe even a chance for new beginnings . . .

Sparks of fear mingled with anticipation flicker in my chest. Annoyingly, I'm coming round to the idea that Mum was right – this event could be something for me to look forward to. After all, what else do I have going on in my life right now? Sweet FA.

I have the sudden panicked thought that I might not be able to retrieve the email. That it could have been permanently deleted. I quicken my pace again, turning into Brock Street, welcoming the shade of the narrow road. Finally, I reach the Royal Crescent with its familiar sight of tourists and residents relaxing and picnicking on the jewel-green lawns. I suddenly can't wait to get into my flat, have a cool shower, crack open that bottle of rosé and start planning.

Half an hour later, I'm doing just that, curled up on the sofa with my laptop. The windows are open, letting in an early-evening breeze along with the sound of laughter, traffic and the distant bassline thump of music. Thankfully, the invitation was still sitting there in the deleted folder, waiting to be transferred back to my inbox.

With a nervous skip of excitement, I open the email and read the details. The reunion is going to be held at the school itself, which is more than a little nerve-racking. After I left the place fifteen years ago, I was certain I'd never set foot in there again. Not after what happened. The event isn't until the end of November. It's September now, so that gives me two months to prepare. Time to lose a little weight and get my confidence back. I could restart my direct debit for the gym. Book some facial treatments with Samantha at the salon and get my blonde highlights back on track.

The invitation was emailed from a former classmate, Georgia Cavendish. I didn't know her that well back then. All I remember is that she was super-posh and lived on one of the roads above Sandbanks Peninsula – one of the most expensive pieces of land in the country, if not the world. I went to one of her parties in Year 7, before she became more picky about who received an invitation. The party was held in her fancy house with marquees on the lawn, security on the gates and fireworks at the end of the night. All very awe-inspiring to a scholarship girl like me who grew up in a rented flat by the side of a busy main road outside Westbourne. The same flat Mum lives in today.

There's a link to a Facebook group. I'm only on Facebook to please Mum – a way for her to keep tabs on my life – but I think she's disappointed with my lack of engagement on there. I don't think I've looked at it in over a year, but I open up the site straightaway and sign in, trying to get my bearings. After clicking on notifications, I scroll down until I find the invitation to the *Class of 2008 West Cliff School Reunion* group. I push away all my doubts, take a breath, exhale and press *accept*.

The Facebook group header picture is a photograph of the school. My breath catches as my eyes rake over the image of the three-storey grey stone building with its mullioned windows, stone balustrades and sloping green lawns. How can so much emotion be evoked by a photo? I scroll down to the chat, wondering if I should contribute, or simply lurk. My name has now been added to the group, so everyone will be able to see that I'm attending. I go back up and click on the list of members, my brain scrabbling to make connections for a few of them, but curious to see what they're all doing now, to see what they look like, where they live. I guess they can all make assumptions about me now too. I take a gulp of cold wine, wondering if I might have made a terrible mistake. But what will it look like now if I unjoin the group?

As instructed by the pinned post at the top of the page, everyone has made a welcome post, some giving their maiden names if they're married. No need for me to do that – I was Chloe Flynn back then until I married and became Chloe Culleton. But now I'm Flynn again. Before I can change my mind, I start typing:

> Chloe Flynn:
>
> Hey, hope everyone's well. Looking forward to catching up at the reunion.

It looks a bit formal, so I add an exclamation mark. Now it looks too chirpy. I hate the way everything on social media has to be so fake and smiley – like we're all children's TV presenters. But if you don't end everything with an exclamation mark or an excited emoji, you come across like a serial killer. I press send with the exclamation mark in place, cringing slightly. Is this how it's going to be now? Me second-guessing every interaction with these people I haven't seen in fifteen years? I refuse to obsess about this. They can take me as they find me.

I close the laptop, get to my feet and head over to the window with my glass of wine, sipping as I watch the clusters of people lounging on the grass. Friends and families. What I wouldn't give for some of that comforting security. A husband to love, children, a group of friends I can count on . . . I sniff away the self-pity and return to my laptop – this black metal slab that's suddenly become a portal into my past.

The reunion is an opportunity to reconnect with old friends – there weren't that many, only a couple really – but, if I'm honest, those fragile friendships aren't the only reason I'm hopeful for what the reunion might bring. No. There's another reason. The only reason I'd *consider* putting myself through the torture of seeing those people again. One that I haven't even allowed myself to think about until now. And his name is Nathan Blake.

Chapter Four

Zero on the clock. My toes grip the starting block as I focus on the calm blue, ready to cut through the glassy surface and follow the black line. Ready to channel my whole being. To be the best. Right now, nothing else matters. Only the water and my body. Nerves twist my stomach. But they're good nerves. Not the terrifying kind that cling to me every second I'm away from the pool. My school life outside the water has become nothing but constant fear and the desperate yearning to be back here on the starting block.

All external sounds recede. Just the steady whoosh of blood in my ears. My muscles and sinews strain. My ears are cocked for the beep.

When it finally comes, it's a release. I leap, bubbles grazing my skin, streaming. Nothing matters but the here and now, the steady kick, kick, kick, the muted sound beneath the water and the roar of air as I surface. A rhythm that's as familiar as my heartbeat.

Almost at the wall, I sense the others turning before me, but that's part of my plan. Conserve my energy for the first hundred metres and then let fly for the final hundred. I keep my nerve and try not to panic as the others pull away. My time will come.

And it does.

After my second turn, I dig deep and give it everything. These girls want to win. But I need *to win. Swimming is all I have. It's what got me here. It's what keeps me sane. Everything else is bullshit.*

My lungs are on fire, but after a brutal two hundred metres, I'm first to touch the final wall. I stare up at the board to confirm, and there it is – my name in first place. There's no doubt now that I'll be the one chosen to represent the school.

I'm happy, of course I am. It's what I wanted. But I was happier still on the starting block when the clock was at zero and the race was still ahead of me. When I didn't have to get out of the water and into the changing rooms to face them all. Those girls. Those creatures who feel like a different species to me with their vicious words and sneering glances. I drop beneath the surface, savouring these last precious seconds of peace even as the familiar sick feeling spreads through me at the thought of having to endure the rest of the day.

Chapter Five

DEAN

Pushing my hair back from my face with both hands, I let out a frustrated growl. I'm sitting at the small black kitchen table in my flat, sorting out my bills into three piles – pay now, pay later, and pay when and if a miracle occurs. I've been putting off doing it for a while, but worrying about it has almost been worse than doing it. I needed to know just how bad things are. And the answer is – *bad*.

The thing that pisses me off most is that I'm a good person. At least, I've always tried to be. I take care of those I love, I'm a loyal friend, I pay my taxes . . . and yet it hasn't made any difference. There are ruthless bastards out there who always manage to get away with everything. Maybe I've been doing life wrong all this time. I always expected to be treated how I treat others, but I keep getting shat on from a great height. There's so much fury building up inside my chest right now, I think I might explode.

Ellis is in bed, but he's already been up four times this evening – for water, for a wee, to tell me he can't sleep, and for a cuddle. I'm expecting a fifth visitation any minute now. I'm always careful not to let him see how much pressure I'm under. To show him my gentle side, and not the part of me that's being pushed to the edge. The part that makes me want to rip up these bills and upend this table. The part of me that wants to smash up the kitchen and yell until my throat is raw.

The buzzer goes and I take a breath to calm myself. I'm not expecting anyone. I stand and head to the front door, hoping the buzzer isn't going to get Ellis out of bed again. I press the intercom. 'Hello?'

'Dean?'

'Yeah, who's this?'

'Ollie Tate. Can I come in?'

Damn. Ollie's the electrician I used on the Tamber project. The project I haven't been paid for. I buzz him in, wondering what he's going to say. I'm not too happy about him coming here while Ellis is at home. Ollie's generally a chilled kind of guy, but whenever money's involved things can get heated.

'All right, mate?' Ollie stands outside my front door. He's not smiling or catching my eye.

'Yeah, you?'

'Can I come in?'

I hesitate. 'You can, but my lad's in bed, so you'll have to talk quietly.'

He nods and follows me into the lounge. Thankfully, there's no sign of Ellis, so I'm hoping he's fallen asleep at long last.

I gesture to the sofa.

'I'm not staying,' Ollie says tersely. 'Me and my crew need to be paid. It's been over four months now.'

'I'm sorry, Ollie,' I say, meaning it. 'You know I got shafted on that project. I'm sorting it out. I just need another month or two.'

'That's what you said last month. And the one before that.' Ollie's face is flushed. He's squaring his shoulders, his fingers flexing and clenching by his side.

My heart rate speeds up in response. I'm not going to let this get out of hand. Not here. Not now. And especially because none of this is my fault.

I've worked on building sites since I was eighteen. Then, when I was twenty-three, I got up the courage to apply for a business loan from the bank to do up a 1940s bungalow that needed complete modernisation. I did most of the work myself, bringing in the trades when I needed them. It was hard work, and I made a lot of mistakes, but I also learnt a lot. I made fourteen grand on that bungalow – not a massive amount when you factor in the time I spent on it, but enough to give me the confidence to keep going.

I flipped two more properties, but it was really hard, and I still didn't manage to make the big bucks I was hoping for. So, eight years ago, I set up my own building firm instead, working on other people's properties – extensions, loft conversions, bathrooms, kitchens. All of the money with none of the risk. Until recently.

A month before my mum died, my business went under because a wealthy client refused to pay up, citing substandard work. But that was a lie; my work is always immaculate. I've since heard that he's pulled the same stunt on other builders. The man is a multimillionaire, but he's also a cheating, stealing scumbag.

I always make sure clients put down a deposit at the start of a project, and then pay the rest in stages so I don't get hugely out of pocket. But then Chris Tamber approached me. He asked me to build a huge lodge-style three-bedroom annex in the grounds of his mansion in Branksome Park – a property worth in excess of four million pounds. He said he'd pay me a cash bonus of thirty grand if I completed the lodge by Easter. He paid the deposit the same day I invoiced him, so I assumed everything would be fine. That he was good for the rest of the money.

Tamber didn't pay the next instalment, or the next. He kept saying he'd get it to me, but that he was out of the country, or that he had personal issues, or that he had to move some funds. I should have stopped work there and then. Waited for the outstanding amount. But he was always so reasonable, so complimentary about the work. I kept thinking of the bonus and what it could do for me and Ellis. I was going to take some time off and book us an amazing holiday – maybe a safari – and put the rest into a savings account. I was an idiot to trust Tamber just because he's rich and charming. He didn't make his money by being nice or playing fair.

We finally had a showdown at the almost-completed site where he pointed out non-existent problems and said the workmanship was shoddy. He said he wasn't going to give me another penny and that he was going to sue me for the deposit he'd already paid. Of course, he didn't say any of this in front of my employees or the other trades, because he knew they'd kick off. He waited for an evening when everyone else had gone home. When I was the only one left on site. Tamber is a crook. I poured my heart into that project, hoping he'd recommend me to his wealthy friends. The place was stunning, and everyone who worked on it was blown away by the high specs and beautiful finishes.

It makes me sick to think about the stress that man has put me through over the past few months, all while I was caring for, and then grieving for, my mum. Since that last conversation, I've tried to meet with him again to get him to see reason. Twice he agreed to meet me, and twice he didn't show up. Now he won't even return my calls.

I suppose inheriting Mum's house has come at the best time for me financially. It has the potential to balance everything back to zero if I sold it. That would fix a lot. I'd be able to pay off all the trades and part of my bank loan. But why should I have to give up my family home – my son's future inheritance – because of a greedy, immoral bastard who thinks he can treat me like shit? Who thinks he can get away with stealing my livelihood?

First things first: I need to calm Ollie down. The look on his face matches the rage thundering in my chest whenever I think of Tamber's arrogant dismissal of me and my work.

'I know you're pissed off,' I say, 'but I'm going to visit Tamber this week. Get him to pay up.'

'How are you gonna do that?' Ollie snaps, his face wrinkling in contempt. 'He's already refused to pay, hasn't he? Look, I know you've got a cash flow problem because of that prick, but I need to pay my crew *now* and I need to pay my bills. You promised he was good for the money, but he wasn't. So I'm holding you responsible.'

I nod. 'Message received. I'm sorting it, okay? If he won't pay up, I'll take him to court for the money.'

Ollie shakes his head, not buying my assurances. 'Not good enough. How long will that take?' He scowls. 'You do what you've gotta do with Tamber, but I need paying this week, Dean. I'm serious. By Friday lunchtime, okay?'

I can't agree to that timescale. I just don't have the money. I try another tack. 'Okay, look, if I do have to take him to court, can I count on you to back me up that the work we did was good? If we stick together, he won't be able to get away with it.'

Ollie flushes and looks at his feet.

'Why are you looking like that?' I ask, getting a bad feeling. 'You know the work we did was good, right?'

He glances up at me, shifting from one foot to the other. 'I shouldn't be telling you this, but one of Tamber's guys caught up with me on another site. He said that if I sided with you on this, he'd make sure my business failed.'

'What the hell!' I cry, immediately worrying that I might have woken Ellis. I try to lower my voice, but fury is spilling out of me. 'I don't believe this!' I run my hands over the top of my head and start pacing the small kitchen.

Ollie raises his hands. 'I know. But I can't take the risk, mate. He's connected.'

'So you're just going to let him ruin me?' I demand.

'Sorry, Dean. I'm caught in the middle here. I just need you to pay up, that's all. I've got a family.'

I shake my head. 'If he's got to you, he'll have spoken to all the other trades too . . .' My brain starts making connections.

Ollie shrugs, embarrassed. 'Probably.'

'Jesus. He's got himself a three-hundred-thousand-pound lodge for thirty grand.'

'It's pretty bad.' He nods, but then his face hardens. 'So, by Friday, Dean, yeah?'

I don't reply. I just show him to the door, my brain speeding.

After what he's just told me, I can't blame Ollie for being scared of Tamber. But I don't know how he can expect me to pay him anything. Tamber's the man he should be visiting, not me. I'm in the same boat as Ollie. But, of course, I'm a softer touch than Tamber. I'm the mug who let him take advantage. I don't know what I'm going to do about Ollie and the rest of them. I just don't have the cash right now. Mum's house is still in probate. I barely have enough money to cover next month's bills and this flat is already mortgaged up to the max.

There's no way on God's earth I'm letting Tamber get away with this. I'm getting what I'm owed. Chris Tamber is going to regret what he's done to me.

He's going to pay. One way or another.

Chapter Six

CHLOE

It's another four days before I check the Facebook group again. I didn't want to spend the whole weekend obsessing over it, worrying about whether anyone had replied to my post or not, so I made a deal with myself that I'd wait until at least the middle of the week to look. Well, it's Tuesday, and that's almost the middle of the week, right?

My heart is in my throat as I check the notifications on my phone and see that three people have commented on my post. Three of the *worst* people.

Abigail Matthews:

Omg! Chloe Flynn! Hey, Zara and Gemma have you seen who's coming? It's Fishy Flynn.

Zara Wickes:

No way! Hey Fishy 🙂

Abigail Matthews:

So funny!

Gemma Radcliffe:

Fishy Flynn! That takes me back.

Abigail Matthews:

Hey, Chloe, you know we're only joking. Can't wait to see you!

My blood heats at their comments. I'd stupidly hoped they might have grown out of it by now, but their 'fun' comments were always designed to be just on the right side of bitchy, so they could say they were *only joking* or *Oh, God, Chloe, you take everything so seriously*. It's their clever trap. One that's hard to escape from. If I don't attend the reunion now, they'll say it's because I'm over-sensitive and don't know how to have fun. But it's hard to be light-hearted when there are three of them and one of me.

I should have known they'd resurrect that horrible nickname. Because I got into the school on a swimming scholarship, they thought it was hilarious. They would make a pretence of sniffing whenever I came into the room. *Can you smell something fishy?* they'd ask, making the boys laugh. It started back when we were eleven, but continued right the way through school.

We're in our thirties now, for goodness' sake. It's pathetic. I'm not going to let them put me off going. I refuse to be intimidated. It's not just them and their fancy clique who went to West Cliff. I spot a notification in Messenger and click on it, wondering if it's Mum. She doesn't often message me on Facebook, but maybe she's somehow seen that I've accepted the reunion invitation. This is one time when I'll be glad to chat to my mother – even if it's to hear her pick apart my life choices. At least I know she loves me.

The message isn't from Mum, it's from one of my old school friends.

> Harriet Walsh:
>
> Hey Chloe, how are you? So pleased you're coming to the reunion. Just thought I'd private message to say ignore those idiots. Abi and her cronies look like complete losers with their passive-aggressive shit.

Now there's a blast from the past. Harriet Walsh! I can't deny that it feels great to have an ally against Abigail and her clique. I'm grateful to Harriet for getting in touch. It was so thoughtful of her to realise that I'd be feeling uncomfortable after their bitchy comments. I type back a reply.

> Harriet! It's been so long. Lovely of you to message. Yeah, I wasn't planning on replying. Not sure why I posted anything in the first place. Am I mad to be thinking of going? Are you going?
>
> Yeah, I'm going. Don't worry, it'll be great. You have to come. Don't let Abi put you off.
>
> Okay, as long as you're going to be there too! I can't wait to catch up!
>
> Same 🙂

I live in Bath these days. Are you still in Bournemouth?

Yep, still here. Look, I know it's short notice but I don't suppose you're around this evening? I've just been to an exhibition in Birmingham and could stop off in Bath for a quick drink on my way home? No worries if you're busy.

I'd love that. Thanks Harriet xx

Two and a half hours later, I'm sitting in a bar on Milsom Street sipping a G&T, waiting for Harriet to arrive. My stomach knots in a weird mixture of anxiety and anticipation at our imminent meeting; at this reignition of a past I thought I'd left behind. I finally spot her glancing up at the sign before walking in, and my nerves spike. She still looks the same, with her light brown hair and green cat eyes, only smarter, more polished. I wonder what she's going to think of me. I run a hand over my freshly washed hair and then lift it in greeting.

'Oh, wow, you literally haven't changed!' Harriet says with a laugh as she comes over. She leans in to kiss my cheek and stares at me again. 'Except for the blonde hair. It suits you.'

I'm staring back. 'It's crazy to see you as a grown-up. In my head, you're still sixteen.'

'You too.' She grins. 'And now you don't have wet hair!'

'I don't miss that,' I reply with a shudder, remembering early-morning winter swim sessions with not enough time to dry my hair before registration. I was always shivering back then. By the time my hair dried, it was lunchtime and I was already back in the pool. I loved swimming, but the downside was feeling cold and damp afterwards. That, and having to put up with the rest of the swim team, who all thought they were better than me. Harriet and Jas were my salvation throughout school.

She orders a dry ginger ale and I pass her a menu. 'Have you eaten?' I ask.

'Actually, no. Apart from an apple in the car. I'm starving.'

'They do tapas here, if you like?'

'I like very much,' she replies, her eyes shining.

I order at the bar and return with more drinks, my mind buzzing with memories. Seeing Harriet after all this time is bringing up events and incidents that I haven't thought about in years. Like the time Jas made us all steal a lipstick from Superdrug, or the summer after exams when the two of them went to Greece without me.

'You're married now, aren't you?' Harriet asks as I sit back down. 'Any kids?'

'No kids, and I'm actually divorced,' I clarify, with a twinge of sadness.

'Oh, sorry . . . or congratulations?' She offers a tentative smile.

'Half and half,' I reply, tilting my hand back and forth. 'It was terrible at the time, but I'm okay now. How about you?'

'I never got married, but I've got my eye on someone,' she replies cagily.

'Ooh, what's this "someone" like?'

'Arrogant and annoying, but I think that's part of the appeal.'

I nod with a knowing smile. 'Why are we always drawn to those types? You know what, the next man I go for is going to be someone *nice*.'

'But hot,' Harriet adds.

'Definitely – if such a man exists.' We clink glasses and I feel a sudden pang of regret over our years of lost friendship. 'I'm sorry I never kept in touch.'

Harriet tilts her head. 'I know. Me too.'

'I just . . . I don't know . . . after everything that happened at the end of school, I wanted to start fresh. But I regret not staying in contact with you and Jas. Do you two still see each other?'

'Me and Jas? Most weeks, yes.'

'Oh, wow.' I'm surprised to feel a twinge of jealousy that Harriet stayed friends with Jasmine Trelawney. The three of us were so close back then, until everything went wrong. I manage a smile, remembering Jasmine's fiery personality. 'Is she still causing trouble?'

'You know it.' Harriet shakes her head. 'If there's drama, Jas will find it. Although she's married now and works as a legal secretary, so she has to at least try to be sensible during working hours.'

'Do you remember that time she and Abigail got into a fight in Year 9?' A memory pops up of Jas and Abigail in the girls' toilets, shoving one another against the sinks. 'What was it about?'

'I can't even remember,' Harriet replies. 'Hopefully there won't be a repeat performance this year.'

'Can you imagine?'

The next hour and a half passes too quickly as Harriet fills me in on what some of our other classmates are doing now. Most are living fabulously wealthy and successful lives, as I knew they would be. Harriet comes from a regular middle-class family whose parents scrimped to send her to West Cliff. 'I think I'm quite a disappointment to them,' she jokes.

'I doubt that,' I reply, nibbling on an onion ring. 'What is it you do these days?'

'Interior design,' she replies. 'I beautify the homes of Bournemouth and Poole's rich and famous.'

'Oh, that's right,' I say. 'I remember you were always good at arty stuff. Don't tell my mum – she'll want to go into partnership with you. You went to Bournemouth Arts Uni, didn't you?'

Harriet nods, a faraway look in her eyes. 'Best days of my life. Did you do anything with your swimming after you left school? Did you compete at all? I did google you, but—'

'No.' I cut her off. 'I'd had enough of swimming by then. I did some lifeguarding for a while, but I actually ended up going into banking, if you can believe it.'

'Really? But you hated maths!' Harriet laughs.

'The irony,' I reply, with a sudden heaviness in my soul. It isn't exactly my dream job – working behind a glass counter, paying in other people's money and handing it out. Being trained up to give out loans and sell insurances. Maybe if numbers were my thing, I'd enjoy it more. Swimming was my only real love. But that ship sailed years ago. I'm not going to moan about my job though. I don't want Harriet to think my life is completely tragic.

'Anyway.' She glances at her phone. 'It's . . . wow, it's almost ten. I should get going if I want to get home before midnight. I know it's only a couple of hours' drive, but it's been a long day.'

'You're welcome to stay over?' I offer.

'Thanks, but I've got a client meeting tomorrow morning.' She gets to her feet. 'I can't believe we didn't even have time to bitch about Abigail Matthews properly.'

'We'd need a couple more hours for that,' I reply, trying not to think about that horrible catty thread on Facebook.

'And the rest,' Harriet agrees, shrugging on her jacket. 'You should spend a few days in Bournemouth over the reunion weekend. I guess you'll stay with your mum, right? We can arrange to go out one night beforehand. I'll message Jas to come along too.'

'That would be amazing!' I reply, meaning it, feeling grateful that Harriet still wants to keep in contact. That she's welcoming me back into our old friendship group. This evening has been more enjoyable than I imagined. 'Are you parked nearby?' I ask, standing up.

'Broad Street.' She points in the opposite direction to where she needs to go.

'I'll walk with you,' I offer, worried she might get lost.

We chatter non-stop on the way back to the car and it feels so nice. I can't remember when I last felt this comfortable with a friend. The belly laughs and the easiness that comes with knowing someone since you were a kid. It's a different kind of friendship to the ones I've made as an adult.

After we've said our goodbyes, I amble back home, my footsteps ringing out along the quiet streets, my mind awash with memories of being a teenager. Of early-morning training sessions, and feeling exhausted during class. Of navigating friendships and enemies. Rich kids like Abigail and a few poor kids like me. Of teachers pushing us to achieve and do better than some of us were capable of. They were messy, scary, frantic days and I don't miss them at all. But I'm glad I've reconnected with Harriet, and it'll be good to see Jas again.

Arriving back at my dark, empty flat, I'm hit with a pang of loneliness. I have the notion that maybe staying on in Bath after splitting from Ben wasn't such a great idea. Although the thought of living any closer to my mother is enough to put the kibosh on all thoughts of moving back to Bournemouth. I shake my head, imagining her popping round every day to offer up new observations about my life and how I'm doing everything wrong. With a shudder, followed by a flash of guilt at thinking so badly of her, I turn on the hall light and throw my keys on the wooden hall table with a clatter.

I make myself a green tea and sit on the couch with my phone. Just because I'm not going to post anything else on the reunion page doesn't mean I'm not going to stalk it relentlessly. I open up the group page, where the most recent post makes my pulse quicken.

Abigail Matthews:

Hey guys, is there anyone else we've forgotten to invite?

What about Nathan Blake? I can't find him on Facebook. We should send him an invitation.

Gareth Moore:

Nathan moved to New Zealand with his family in the middle of Year 10, I think. Didn't Mark Steeples used to hang round with him?

Mark Steeples:

Sorry, lost touch with him.

Abigail Matthews:

Anyone else have any contact details for Nathan?

No one else has replied to Abigail, and she posted it almost three hours ago. Should I even bother going if Nathan's not going to be there? He was always my crush, the one who got away. I don't know why I'm even thinking about him – he's probably married with kids by now. Nathan Blake was the tall, dark and moody boy that everyone secretly fancied. I never knew him that well, but I always hoped something might happen between us. I caught him looking at me a few times and if I'd been braver, I would have spoken more than two words to him. But I wasn't, so I missed my opportunity.

I'd been wondering if the reunion might give me a second shot. My cheeks heat up as I remember an embarrassing incident at the end of class where Nathan asked to borrow one of my textbooks. Abigail noticed us talking and she came over and warned him not to borrow anything of mine because it would smell of fish. Everyone laughed and started chanting *Fishy Flynn*. Nathan gave me a sympathetic smile, but I left the classroom feeling humiliated, taking the textbook with me.

Even if he does decide to come along to the reunion, it's obvious that Abigail's set her sights on him. Why else would she be so keen to track him down? I wouldn't stand a chance, with her and her friends around. If they're anything like they used to be – which it's clear they are – they wouldn't let me get anywhere near him without trying to make me look bad. And why would Nathan be interested in me when he could have perfect Abigail Matthews?

I drop my phone on to the sofa in disgust and lean back against the cushions. Why the hell am I letting that girl get to me? I feel like I'm sixteen years old all over again, letting my insecurities stop me from going after what I want.

I make a deal with myself – if, by some miracle, Nathan Blake attends the reunion and he's single, I'll talk to him. Maybe I'll even make a move on him, or at least drop heavy hints that I'm interested. You only live once, right? My phone buzzes, jolting me from my thoughts.

It's an email. Probably something boring. I open it, my thoughts straying to the memory of Nathan. But I'm brought back to the present with an ugly thud when I read what's written on the screen:

Stay at home

From: No Reunion

To: Chloe Flynn

Don't even think of coming to the reunion. Nobody wants you there and you'll be sorry if you do.

Bloody hell! I almost drop my phone.

I reread it in disbelief. With shaking fingers, I click on the sender's name to see if there's any clue about who it might be – not that I'm expecting whoever it is to advertise themselves. The email address is: noreunion23@gmail.com. There's probably no way of tracing it unless I call the police. Adrenaline flows hot in my veins. Do I want to call the police? Not really. Should I reply? Ask them to explain themselves? Maybe that's what they want – to anger or scare me. Are they waiting for me to respond right now? I shouldn't give them the satisfaction.

Could it be Abi or one of her horrible friends? Surely not. But she obviously still likes Nathan. Maybe she thinks I might be some kind of competition. Could she really be as much of a bitch today as she was back then? Would she stoop to something so nasty as a threatening email? If not her, then who? This is crazy. Who on earth would do such a thing?

What about my ex, Chris? He was pretty pissed off when we broke up. But that was years ago, and I can't imagine he'd be the type to resort to anonymous threats. Although I guess a lot can change in fifteen years. It must be somebody from school who knows about the reunion. But I'm not in touch with any of my old classmates on email, so how would they have got hold of my address? Unless . . .

I open up the original email invitation and my heart drops. It's as I suspected – Georgia copied everyone in to the invitation without hiding our email addresses. So the message could have been sent by anyone on the list. Pretty sure that's a violation of our privacy, but I'm not about to call Georgia out on it. It's done now. Besides, knowing who else is on the list, I can imagine several of them have already contacted Georgia to tell her how unprofessional it was of her to do that.

I press a hand to my heart to try to calm my breathing. Seeing Harriet this evening has already sent my thoughts racing backwards. I was relieved that we still clicked but now getting this horrible message has sent me into a spiral of anxiety again. I toss my phone back on to the sofa, get to my feet and walk to the window, staring out across the dark lawns towards the twinkling lights of the city. Normally this view calms me. Not this evening.

When I accepted the invitation, I had stupidly and naively hoped that I'd be able to keep those dark times buried. But it's clear now that someone out there doesn't want me to forget. They're trying to drag me back. To scare me. The question is . . . *who*? Who wants to rake up the past? There's only one person who truly knows what went on, but surely it can't be them. It *can't* be.

As I gaze out into the inky night, my skin starts to prickle. What if whoever sent that email is out there right now, watching me? I glance up and down at the road, and at the parked cars below. I don't see anyone, but that doesn't mean they're not there, lurking in the shadows, staring up at my frightened face. Laughing at me. With clammy hands, I tug the curtains closed, my breathing ragged, my stomach tight with fear.

That email was designed to unsettle me, to scare me. Well, it's certainly done its job. I should ignore it, delete it. Push it from my mind. But that's easier said than done. Those words on the screen are burned into my brain.

My apartment is usually my sanctuary, the place I retreat to when everything outside feels too much. But tonight it feels unfamiliar. Violated. I shiver and wrap my arms around myself, suddenly feeling very cold and very alone.

Chapter Seven
DEAN

I walk away from the school gates quickly, with my head down. I don't have time to catch any of the other parents' attention this morning. It's Ellis's first day back after the summer holidays. He was so excited this morning that he woke up at five thirty, chattering away about how he can't wait to see his best friends, Isla and Grace. And how none of them are going to be babies in Reception anymore, but big children in Year 1.

My van's parked round the corner. Once we move into Mum's house, we'll be able to walk to school rather than fight the rush-hour traffic. It will be the same walk I did with my school friends every day. I like the thought of that for Ellis, even though everything's still very much up in the air. Familiar knives of panic stab my chest at the prospect of losing my family home. I can't let that happen. I *won't* let it happen.

I slide into the driver's seat and grasp the steering wheel, anxious at the thought of what I'm about to do. But what other choice do I have? I have to at least try.

Heading out of Westbourne towards Bournemouth town centre, I'm hot and uncomfortable in my dark suit. It's the only one I own, reserved for weddings, funerals and other rare occasions. I don't have much call to dress smartly in my line of work. I turn up the air-con and try to marshal my thoughts, but my brain feels hectic, my mind unable to hold on to anything.

A Nissan Micra cuts into my lane on the roundabout, forcing me to brake. Without thinking, I bash my horn, feeling instantly guilty when I see it's a lady around my mum's age. I pull back and hope I haven't unnerved her. As she waves an apology, I feel like such a dick letting my stress get the better of me. Turning me into one of those aggressive drivers everyone hates. With a few deep breaths, I try to get a handle on my emotions, needing to be the one in control today.

I turn off towards the Lansdowne, where Chris Tamber's office is situated. We have a meeting scheduled for nine fifteen. Only he doesn't know the meeting is with me. He thinks it's with a man called George Solomon who wants to discuss leasing two floors of office space for his financial firm. I made up George Solomon to get the meeting. There's no way Tamber would let the real me enter his building, let alone his private office.

It's five past nine. I don't drive into the car park in case he looks out of the window and recognises my van. Instead, I park on the road and feed the meter. One hour should give me enough time. I'll be lucky if he lets me stay beyond a minute. I'm going in there to appeal to his better nature – if he has one – hoping he'll be reasonable. If we can just get the chance to talk face to face like decent human beings then maybe we can sort something out. Although I'm desperate more than hopeful, remembering how our last face-to-face meeting went. But that time I was caught off guard. This time I'm prepared.

I walk across the visitor car park and head to the entrance of the iconic Art Deco-style Bournemouth office block – a twelve-storey wall of curved smoked glass. As I go through the revolving door, finding myself in a vast triple-height foyer, I tell myself to be calm, confident and friendly. Don't let him rile me. I already know he's an arsehole. I just have to come away with a better outcome than I have at the moment. The man has cheated me. If he has any conscience whatsoever, surely he'll be glad to come to a compromise. It's not as if he can't afford it.

I head over to a curved white-onyx desk, behind which are three reception staff. Two women are currently on phone calls, and a man in a suit nods as I approach.

'Hi, I've got a meeting with Chris Tamber at nine fifteen,' I say.

'With Mr Tamber? Can I take your name, please?' he asks in a bored tone.

'Uh, D— George Solomon.'

'Okay, if you could sign in . . .' the man says, sliding a clipboard across the counter along with a visitor badge that I clip on to my lapel.

Thankfully, I remember to sign in as George Solomon.

'If you wait over there, someone will come down to get you.' He indicates a cluster of velvet sofas and leather club chairs.

'Thanks,' I reply, heading over to the seating area and glancing at the bank of elevators. I pour myself a cup of water from the cooler, grateful for the opportunity to ease my dry throat. One of the walls is covered in sepia photos of old Bournemouth, including a picture of this office block when it was first built. I run my gaze over all the images and can't help wondering how many of these long-since-dead people in the photos found themselves in a similar predicament to me – shafted by a rich, powerful man who thought he could get away with it.

After a while, a lift pings. I turn as one of the doors opens.

A young woman in a beige trouser suit, her shiny hair clipped up in a ponytail, steps out. 'Mr Solomon?'

I nod. My mouth suddenly dry again. I drain the water in my cardboard cup, crumple it and drop it into the metal bin.

'Great.' She smiles. 'I'm Melanie, Mr Tamber's assistant. I'll take you up.'

I follow her into the lift, where we make small talk about the mild September weather and I comment on the historic photos on the wall.

'Did you know that Mr Tamber's great-grandfather built this block back in the thirties?'

'I didn't.'

'Yes.' She nods. 'His family built a lot of commercial buildings here and in London. They were instrumental in bringing a lot of prosperity to the area.'

Yeah, and taking it away, too, I think to myself.

'Mr Tamber always has his eye on new projects. The office space he's going to show you today is world-class in terms of facilities and views. We're excited for you to see it.'

I realise too late that I probably shouldn't have made George Solomon into such a big shot. Tamber's going to be more than a little disappointed when he sees that it's me and not some potential rich client. That's not going to put him in the best mood to hear my pleas.

The lift door opens and sweat starts to prickle beneath my shirt. I blink and take a breath. I can't waste this opportunity. I need to remain calm and collected, but the more I have that thought, the more nervous I become. My head swims and my vision blurs for a moment until I take a breath and tell myself to get it together.

Melanie leads me along a wide, plush corridor with marble flooring, glass globe ceiling lights and green leafy plants in square bronze-coloured pots. She points out various offices along the way, all humming with activity behind black-framed interior windows. But I'm too wired to concentrate on her words. This meeting could change the course of my fortunes. I need it to be successful.

'Here we are,' Melanie says, rapping on an opaque glass door and opening it without waiting for a reply from within.

Chris Tamber is sitting behind an enormous polished dark-wood desk. His brown hair is neat, he's freshly shaved and his dark eyes glitter with fake friendship as he looks up and smiles. He rises to his feet and comes round the desk to shake my hand. But his smile falters when he registers my face and realises who I am.

'What the hell are *you* doing here?' he barks before turning his irritated gaze on his assistant. 'Mel, why did you let this man in? Where's Mr Solomon?'

I can sense her confusion, but I don't take my gaze off Tamber. His eyes are narrowing like a bird of prey homing in on something.

I hold up my hands. 'Chris, I'm sorry to arrive unannounced, but I think it would be good for both of us if we could have a civil conversation.'

'Melanie, please show Mr . . . Bradley out. There's obviously been a mix-up and I don't want to keep my client waiting.'

'About that . . .' I begin.

Understanding slowly dawns across Tamber's face, followed by a deep red fury. 'You've got to be joking.' He shakes his head and glares at me. 'Do you know how busy I am? How much work I put into prepping for this meeting? You pretended to be *George Solomon*?'

'I made him up, I'm sorry. But you wouldn't take my calls and we need to talk.'

'Melanie, show this man out of the building, please,' Tamber says through gritted teeth, taking a step past me and throwing open the door.

'Just give me two minutes of your time,' I say, unmoving, 'and then I'll leave. Two minutes. Don't say you're too busy because I know you have the time right now.'

Tamber folds his arms, his nostrils flaring. '*One* minute and then I'm calling security. Melanie, you can go.'

'So, um, just to be clear,' she says, 'Mr Solomon is—'

Tamber looks like he's about to explode. 'For Christ's sake, there is no Mr Solomon. You can go, thank you, Mel.'

She flushes and scoots out, her ponytail swinging.

Tamber pushes the door closed behind her. He strides back around his desk and takes a seat, gesturing to me to sit opposite, which I do, relieved to have got past this first hurdle, even if he doesn't exactly seem receptive. 'I'm waiting. Your time's ticking, Bradley.'

His dismissive attitude is even more irritating due to the fact that, at thirty-one, he's a couple of years younger than me. This man was handed all his wealth and opportunity at birth – which is fine, good for him – but it's somehow not enough. He still feels the need to cheat other people out of what's rightfully theirs. He's the worst kind of arrogant, entitled bully.

I take a breath, praying I can convince him to do the right thing. 'I'm sorry you weren't happy with the job I did for you, but that was some of the best work my crew and I have ever done. The craftsmanship was immaculate and—'

'No, it wasn't,' he says coldly.

'Chris, we could argue the toss back and forth all day, but—'

'Your finishes were shoddy,' he adds.

'With respect, we hadn't finished the job yet. We had to stop due to lack of payment.'

'Look, Bradley, if I'd known you were such a small-time operation, I'd never have hired you in the first place. My bad. That's your minute up – now, I'd appreciate it if you would please leave.'

'I'm a reasonable man,' I say, trying to keep my voice steady. 'We did a solid job for you. As a gesture of goodwill, I'll accept two-thirds of the final cost. That will allow me to at least pay the guys their wages. It's not fair to make them wait for their money. We all have families to support. I'm a single dad with a young son.'

'You should've thought about that before you screwed up the job,' Tamber says with a slow blink of his eyes. 'I'm not a charity.'

I'm trying so hard not to react. Not to get up in his face and lay the guy out with a fist to his nose. But it's taking every ounce of self-control I possess. We're evenly matched in size, both over six feet, both broad-shouldered. His are gym muscles while mine are from hard physical labour. But I have pure rage on my side. Rage that I'm doing my best to shove down.

'Are you using the lodge I built for you?' I ask, my voice stiff. 'Have you had people over to stay in it yet? I'm sure you must have.'

He raises an eyebrow. 'I had to get a team of professionals in to finish the job properly,' he drawls. 'It looks pretty good now. My guests have enjoyed their stays.'

I clench my jaw. 'It was ninety-five per cent finished when we left, Chris. All it needed was a few coats of paint and—'

'It was a mess. No way were you anywhere near finishing it by Easter. I made a judgement call. I was cutting my losses, that's all.'

'Losses? That's a joke. I'm the one with the losses. You never paid the agreed instalments so there were things we weren't able to complete. I work on a payment-by-instalment basis so that I can buy materials and pay my guys their wages. You knew that before we started. Just give me what you owe and we can put this behind us. I'm sure we'll both be happy to do that.'

'You're not getting a penny more, Dean. And I'll tell you what – I'm going to sue you for the deposit I paid. Unless you'd like to return it now and save us both the hassle?'

'Are you fucking joking?' My voice shakes and my face is hot. All my hopes are splintering around me. This man . . . this man cannot be allowed to get away with what he's doing. I can't be the first person he's shafted. And I probably won't be the last. I stand, my whole body tense. 'You're a lying, cheating bastard. I see very clearly how your family made its money. You're criminals.'

'Yeah, okay, Dean,' he says in his irritating drawl. 'This conversation's over. Funny how you're calling me a liar when you're the one who lied your way in here. But I don't suppose I should've expected anything else from a cowboy outfit like yours.' He walks around the desk to open the door and I step up close to him, my fingers itching, curling into fists.

I'm seriously considering punching the guy in his smug face when two dark-suited security guards stride in, take hold of my upper arms, and manhandle me out of the office.

'You better watch your back, Chris,' I grind out. 'I'm not going to forget what you've done. You're a crook.'

As the guards march me back along the corridor, I'm vaguely aware of people in their offices watching my humiliating exit. I don't care about that. I realise I've blown this whole meeting, even though I don't think I could've done anything to change the outcome. Tamber was never going to be reasonable about this. But, then again, after today, neither am I.

Chapter Eight

Once we're all out of the water, Coach congratulates me in front of the others, making me wince. The rest of the team fake being happy for me before heading back to the changing rooms. Coach keeps me talking for a good long while, confirming my place in the short-course championships, critiquing my technique, and giving me pointers for next time. Ways to shave off more seconds and hopefully beat my personal best.

I'm flattered by the special attention, even though I know it will cost me dearly. That every second of praise will be matched with its equivalent in pain. I breathe it all in, knowing that I can do this. I can win all my races and take this dream as far as I want. Is it worth the years of envy and resentment my success has evoked? Is it like this for everyone who's good at something, or have I just been unlucky with my peers? I've thought about what might happen if I threw my races. But I honestly don't think it would make a difference. I'd still be an outcast. And I'd be an outcast who had given up on her dream. I would have nothing at all.

So I take the abuse as the price I have to pay, knowing that as long as my other secret is safe, I can deal with anything.

Chapter Nine

CHLOE

I check my reflection in the bedroom mirror for the tenth time in as many minutes. I know I shouldn't care how I look, but Ben will be here any second, and I need to look as though I have my shit together. I smooth my fingers over my hair, annoyed that my roots are showing, but I still haven't got round to making that hair appointment. Never mind. I'm wearing my new pale-washed jeans – the ones that show off the curves of my bum – and a white lace top with a pretty necklace. My feet are bare except for my favourite pearl-pink nail polish. I'm going for an ethereal, carefree vibe. Even though that's actually the opposite of how I'm feeling inside right now.

With a last spritz of Neroli Portofino body spray, I leave the bathroom and peer out of the kitchen window to the road below. My heart plummets as I see that Ben has arrived with Wendi, who's driving a cherry-red Range Rover Velar. She pulls into a lucky space right outside the front door. Why the hell has she come along?

Ben gets out of the passenger side. He's laughing, his Aviators hiding his eyes. Hopefully, Wendi's just dropping Ben off and isn't planning on coming in too. My whole body tenses when I see her getting out to join him, her dark, wavy hair cascading down her back. I immediately notice that she's wearing the exact same jeans as me. And an almost identical white lace top! Even from here, I can see she looks stunning.

I rush to the bedroom, strip off my jeans and top and panic about what to change into. There are already half a dozen discarded outfits on the bed, and I'm starting to sweat now. *Ugh*. I grab a navy striped T-shirt dress and pull it over my head. It's cute, but I don't feel as sexy in this as I did in my jeans. The doorbell chimes. No time to change now. I don't even know why I'm this bothered. Ben and I are finished, divorced, and he now has a family with the wonderful Wendi. But I think wearing the right outfit is more about me feeling confident than wanting him to still fancy me. I need to appear like I'm rocking the single life. Like I'm happy and relaxed on my own. Without him.

I take a breath and head to the door, wafting a hand under my armpit to try to cool down. I press the buzzer and wait for them to come up, my left eye twitching insanely.

I haven't seen Ben for about five months. Not since I moved into the flat and he came over to clear out some of the furniture left by the tenant. It was an uncomfortable, tense meeting and I wished I'd stayed away to let him get on with it on his own. I've been blindsided today. He called earlier to ask if he could drop round after work with some paperwork for me to sign. Something to do with taking him off the lease on the flat. I checked with my solicitor and she said it was fine. That it was the last thing left to do to make the flat totally mine. But I wish he'd given me a few days' notice before coming over so that I could mentally prepare. Instead, I've been caught on the hop, and I'm flustered.

I hear them outside in the hallway, approaching. A child's cry makes me tense up. Surely they didn't bring their kids too? I don't think I could cope with witnessing their perfect domestic bliss up close. I've only seen Wendi on a couple of previous occasions. Both times were at a distance, and both times I avoided eye contact. I assume she did too. I open the front door, attempting a smile, and there they are – the Culleton family.

'Hi, Ben . . . Wendi,' I say, digging my nails into my thumb-pads. 'Come in.' I hold the door open as Ben nods and steps inside, his young daughter in his arms. She has a thumb jammed in her mouth, her head pressed shyly into his neck. Similarly, Wendi is holding their son, who's attempting to wriggle from her grip.

'Go through to the living room,' I say, following them in a cloud of Wendi's perfume that's contaminating my air. Of course, they would have twins – one of each. How perfectly perfect of them.

'Thanks for doing this,' Ben says airily, as though it's completely normal for him to be in my flat with his new family. 'We're off on holiday for a couple of weeks, and I need to get this document to the solicitor tomorrow morning before we go.'

'It's fine,' I mutter.

Their son stares at me over his mother's shoulder, his wide puppy-dog eyes just like Ben's. I blink and cut eye contact, looking instead at Wendi's pert backside as she sashays across the hall into the living room.

'Oh, it's gorgeous in here.' Her voice is deep and throaty. *Posh*. 'Look at that view, Luca!' She's talking to her infant son, who's still staring at me, or should I say glaring.

I stick out my tongue, and his eyes widen. He frowns and sticks his tongue out too. I can't help grinning at that and his face flushes with the start of a smile before he buries it in his mother's shoulder.

'Where's this document?' I ask, just wanting this over and done with. 'Don't we need to get it witnessed?'

'I'll get Joel and Sash to do it,' he replies. 'They're coming over for dinner later.'

I can't believe how much his casual comment has managed to wound me. Joel and Sasha were our best friends. We were at each other's houses all the time. We holidayed together, got drunk together, were more like family than friends. Now I guess Wendi is Sasha's new best friend. I think the loss of Sasha hurt me almost as much as losing Ben.

I lean over the dining table to sign the form, trying to keep my fingers steady, my mind a blur. All my good intentions to be cool, calm and aloof have flown out the window. I feel winded. Numb. Shocked by the realness of Ben's family. Wendi must think I'm some kind of zombie. After I've signed, Ben asks if he can take the twins, Luca and Olivia, into the kitchen for a glass of water.

'I'll get it,' I say, glad for the opportunity to escape.

'No, it's fine,' Ben replies, as Wendi gives him a pointed look.

I realise they've engineered this so she can be alone with me. Goodness knows why. I can't think of a single thing we could say to each other that wouldn't feel fake or awkward.

'Sorry, I know my being here is a bit weird,' she says, as soon as Ben and the twins have left the room.

I shrug and open my mouth to reply, but nothing comes out. I take a breath instead.

She ploughs on, her voice firm and steady. 'I wanted to come up here with Ben so you and I could . . . clear the air. I hope that's okay?' Her dark eyes are condescendingly kind. She continues, 'I thought, since we live in the same city and we've already crossed paths a few times, well, I thought it would be nice if we could be civil, friendly even. I didn't want any bad feeling between us if we happen to run into one another in social situations.'

What does she think I'm going to do? Start a fight or something? Patronising cow. I want to tell her to piss off, but instead I give a tight nod. 'Sure,' I croak. I clear my throat. 'Sure, of course.' I don't smile and I don't sound enthusiastic, but what does she expect from me?

'Oh, that's such a relief,' she gushes, a genuine smile transforming her from stunning to angelic. 'Thank you.' She pauses and bites her lip before lowering her voice. 'Hope you don't mind me telling you this . . .'

I frown. 'Telling me what?'

'Just in case you're planning to go out . . .'

I shake my head, confused.

'Your dress . . .' she winces. 'I think it's inside out.'

I look down to see that the seams are indeed showing. My cheeks flame. Jesus Christ, I can't even dress myself properly. So much for showing Ben how together my life is. I cringe at the thought of them laughing about it later with Joel and Sasha.

'All good?' Ben has returned, his children now squealing and crawling around the coffee table. He glances at Wendi, who gives him a loving smile and a barely perceptible nod.

I smooth my dress self-consciously. 'Yep, all good,' I say a little too loudly. 'All nice and friendly – aside from the wardrobe malfunction,' I mutter.

Ben's forehead creases in confusion.

'We'd better get these two home before they destroy the place,' Wendi says. 'Nice to finally meet you properly, Chloe.'

I nod, trying not to roll my eyes, unable to utter the words *nice to meet you too*.

'Yeah, thanks for the signature,' Ben adds. 'Appreciate it.'

At last they leave, and I stand in the hall feeling shell-shocked, as though I'm recovering from a heavy night out. Seeing Ben with her, with his children, brings home to me just how much I've lost. Maybe my mother was right. Maybe it would have been better to stick it out with him, despite our lacklustre marriage. Maybe it should have been up to me to put more effort in. To try to make myself more pliant. Or maybe I'm just feeling tired and sensitive today. Lonely.

I shuffle back into the living room in a daze. My goal of getting my life back on track seems further away than ever. I'd hoped that planning to go to the reunion would be the start of something good. Now that seems like it was a ridiculously pathetic hope. It's going to take more than a party to fix my life. Feeling adrift, I sink on to the sofa, trying to steady myself.

How do women like Wendi have their lives so under control? Everything about her was groomed and polished, even her children. Okay, so maybe they were a bit of a handful but that's just kids, isn't it? You want them to have a bit of spirit. I gaze down at my inside-out dress and choke out a bitter laugh, watching a tear splash on to my lap and soak into the material.

I bet everybody loves perfect Wendi. I bet *she* wouldn't get anonymous threatening emails or put her clothes on inside out. I wipe my tears with the back of my hand and let my head drop back against the sofa, staring up at the ceiling and letting my eyes unfocus.

I wonder if I should mention yesterday's threatening email on the reunion chat to try to make whoever sent it feel ashamed. To get some sympathy. I sigh. No. It's not worth it. It would cause too much trouble. I don't want to be at the centre of a drama before I've even arrived at the party. I should just put it out of my head. Although that's easier said than done.

I blocked the email address, but I can't deny that it's deeply unsettled me. I'm actually beginning to wonder if it's still a good idea to attend. Could whoever sent it be dangerous? Would they try to physically harm me? Or is it someone's idea of a hateful prank? This whole reunion thing feels as though it's pulling me back. Like I'm regressing into an insecure teenager all over again. It's bonkers. I shake my head and take a breath. I think I'm getting inside my own head too much. After the horrible email, followed by Ben and Wendi's visit today, my confidence has been knocked. That's all it is. I'll be fine. I can't let one sick individual stop me going to my own school reunion. I've as much right to be there as anyone else.

It'll be good to see everyone again. To get some closure after everything that went on. Then I'll finally be able to put that time behind me and get on with my life. I'm sure that's partly what's been holding me back all these years, what's been messing up my relationships and making me insecure.

I curl my legs under me, daydreaming that Nathan might show up at the reunion. That he and I will talk and he'll tell me how he had a crush on me back then and regretted never acting on it. I allow myself to imagine that he and I will kiss. That he'll fall in love with me and beg me to go back to New Zealand with him. That our lives will be blissful. The past forgotten as we embark on a new life together.

After a while, I reach for my phone to see that Harriet has added me and Jasmine to a group chat on WhatsApp. I skim their conversation about former classmates, chuckling at some of the memories and photos they've added. I was daft to let our friendship slide. At the time, it was the only option. The only way I could move on with my life. After leaving school at sixteen, I wanted to get as far away from the place as possible. Despite close friends like Harriet and Jas, my memories of those days aren't good ones. I shiver as I remember.

Chapter Ten

DEAN

'Dean Bradley?' The man's voice sounds official, even via the intercom.

'Who's this?' I ask, my senses on sudden alert.

'My name's David Hargreaves, I'm a court process officer. Can I come in?'

'A *what*?'

'Law enforcement. Can you let me in, please?'

I freeze for a moment, unsure what to do, but I can't think of any excuse to give, so I buzz him up, my thoughts going straight to Chris Tamber. I bet this has something to do with him. Thankfully, Ellis is at school. A sharp rap on the door makes me jump.

I straighten up, and open the door. The man standing there looks to be in his late fifties or early sixties, with short grey hair. 'Hi, David Hargreaves, court officer,' he repeats, flashing his ID. It looks genuine enough, but I don't have a clue if I'm looking at a fake or at the real thing. Would anybody know the difference?

'Come in,' I offer, not wanting to have this conversation on the landing in case any of my neighbours walk past and think I'm some kind of criminal.

He follows me into the lounge, which is still strewn with breakfast things along with Ellis's toys and Scooby-Doo pyjamas bunched up on the carpet. The two of us normally watch twenty minutes of TV together before school while he's getting ready. Probably not the most perfect parenting routine, but we enjoy it, so I figure what's the harm?

Hargreaves' gaze travels the room before landing back on me. I'm aware that I look a mess in threadbare jogging bottoms and a paint-stained sweatshirt, but I'd planned to start decorating the flat today, to get it ready to rent out, so I'm not going to feel intimidated by this man's appraisal of me.

He clears his throat. 'Like I said at the door, I'm a Bournemouth court officer. I'm here today to serve you with an ex parte non-molestation order.'

Although I've been half expecting something like this for the past few weeks since I paid Tamber a visit, I still can't help the shock that courses through my body. 'You're serving me with an order?'

Hargreaves continues talking. 'An application for an ex parte emergency non-mol was submitted by a Mr Christopher Tamber the day before yesterday—'

'Can you speak English?' I interrupt. 'I'm sorry, but I don't understand any of what you just said.' The only words that are now just filtering into my brain are 'Christopher' and 'Tamber'. I inhale sharply, trying to concentrate, but my mind seems to have seized up.

The man fixes me with a steady gaze, his rheumy blue eyes devoid of emotion. 'A Mr Christopher Tamber has applied to the civil court to issue you with this emergency non-molestation order. All the details are here.' He passes me a sheet of paper.

I don't know whether to be scared or angry. I shouldn't be surprised though – Tamber has already threatened to sue me for the deposit he paid. No way he's getting that back – the money was spent on the materials used to build his lodge. 'Non-molestation?' I shake my head. 'I thought that was something to do with domestic abuse.'

'Non-mols are mainly used in family situations,' Hargreaves explains, 'but they can also be used in the case of employees or neighbours.'

I shake my head and start to pace. 'I can't believe he's the one sticking the order on *me*!' I mutter. 'I did months of building work for the guy and he refused to pay. Just because he's loaded, he thinks he can screw me and my employees over! It's robbery. He's a bully and a thief!'

Hargreaves holds his chin, listening with a blank expression on his face.

I realise my tone is becoming more and more agitated, so I take a breath and lower my voice. 'I mean, yes, I went to his office to ask for payment, but only because he refused to respond to my messages. I asked him nice and calmly to pay me the money he owed. In fact, I even compromised and knocked a third off the total bill, which would have meant I got next to nothing after I'd paid my crew. But he wouldn't listen. He threw me out – well, not him personally, he got his two thug security guards to frogmarch me out of the building. But now he slaps this on me to stop me asking for what's mine.' I take a breath. 'So, what can I do?'

Hargreaves blinks slowly. 'I recommend you try to keep calm, and seek legal advice.' He gives me a nod and turns to leave.

'Keep calm? Legal advice? How much is that gonna cost? I don't have any money because Tamber's got it all!' I pull at my beard, wanting nothing more than to punch something. But that probably wouldn't go down well with a court officer here to witness my anger.

'Look,' Hargreaves says, turning back, a faint trace of pity in his eyes. 'If what you say is true, your best bet is to make a claim through the county court for loss of earnings or non-payment. Unless you've already served papers on him?'

'Not yet.' I sniff. 'But that was going to be my next step.' I wave the sheet of paper at him. 'Does this mean I can't even speak to him anymore?'

''Fraid not. But you'll be able to object to the order. You'll get the chance to present your case to the judge. Tell him why you think it should be thrown out. You didn't lamp him, did you?'

'I never touched him.' Although, thinking back, it was a close call. If those security guards hadn't marched me out of there, I'm pretty sure I would have landed one on Tamber's smug face. No one needs to know that though.

'Well, good,' Hargreaves replies.

I let out a long, slow breath. 'It would suit me fine to never have to go near that arsehole ever again. But he can't get away with not paying what he owes. It's not just my money, it's all my staff, the other guys on the job, so many people are relying on that payment.' I grind my teeth and stop talking. This court officer isn't the one to blame. He's just doing his job. He doesn't need to hear me ranting. But the whole system is ridiculous when it's Tamber issuing me with orders, like I'm the one at fault. 'Anyway, thanks,' I reply with a nod, my mind still whirring. 'It was good of you to explain it to me. I was freaking out there for a minute. Still am, but I appreciate what you said about being given the chance to tell the judge my side.'

'My son was in a similar situation,' Hargreaves replies. 'With the non-payment thing from an old employer.'

'Sorry to hear that,' I say. 'It's grim. What happened with your son?'

Hargreaves looks down at his shoes. 'It's still ongoing,' he replies.

'I hope he gets it sorted,' I add.

'Thank you.' Hargreaves looks up at me again.

'Can I get you a cuppa?' I offer. 'A tea or coffee?'

'That would have been nice, but I can't stop.' He raises his bushy eyebrows. 'Work to do.'

'Sure, yeah, of course. Well, I wish I could say it was nice to meet you.' I manage a bitter smile.

Hargreaves taps a finger to his forehead in a farewell salute, leaving me to stew over Tamber's mission to ruin my life. And what the hell I'm going to do about it.

Chapter Eleven

As I head to the changing rooms, I can't help the shiver that starts in my shoulders and spreads throughout my wet body. I pull the towel closer around me, like it can somehow stop the retribution I'm about to face.

I pause outside the door, but there's no point delaying the inevitable. Head down, I walk in, making straight for the shower, braced for their words. But I quickly realise, with a rush of relief, that the changing room is silent. Empty. There's no one here. Was I talking to Coach for that long? I glance at the clock. Only five minutes have passed. Surely the others wouldn't have showered, dried and changed so quickly. Normally, they dawdle. Laughing and chatting, or torturing me with their sly comments and mocking laughter.

Whatever the reason, I'm grateful for the respite, relaxing my shoulders and rolling my neck from side to side as my shivering eases. The shower is lukewarm as usual, but I don't care. It's a luxury to be in here alone. I hurry, in case they decide to come back. In case SHE decides to come back to make me pay for my win.

I reach over to the hook for my towel, but it's not there. Neither is my swimming costume.

What the hell!

Chapter Twelve

DEAN

'What do you think, Ellis? Do you like it?' I watch his face as his gaze sweeps the room.

Ellis and I are moving into Mum's house today. While he's been at school this week, I've been decorating his new bedroom – my old childhood room.

I'm still trying to work out a way to keep hold of the house and get out of debt. The only way I'm going to be able to manage my immediate bills is to rent out the flat. The house is still in probate but, as an only child and the sole executor of Mum's will, I'm allowed to live in it with Ellis while everything's in process.

My business debts have been cleared with the liquidation of the company, but I still have a few personal loans and overdrafts that I took to tide us over while I was working on the Tamber job. I'm not obliged to pay the other trades as my business has now gone bust, but it doesn't stop me feeling bad about it. Even though this is Tamber's doing and they know it was him who shafted us, it's *my* name that's been tarnished in the industry.

No one will work with me now, so I'm going to have to find another way to earn a living. Maybe as a one-man band. Or maybe I'll be forced to move away from the area and start afresh. The thought of it is giving me a stomach ulcer. Especially with the whole non-molestation order hanging over my head. I was served the non-mol almost two weeks ago and my court date is set for next month, so, until then, I can't even message Tamber or I'll be found in violation. It's doing my head in.

'No way!' Ellis cries, as his eyes alight on the far wall. He races across the room and stares up in wonder. 'The mystery machine! Daddy, it's the mystery machine, and Velma and Fred and Shaggy and Daphne and Scooby!'

'You like it?' My heart lifts at his reaction, letting me push out all the bad stuff for a moment. I managed to find some Scooby-Doo decals on eBay, which I stuck across the wall opposite Ellis's bed. Even though he was used to staying here when Mum was alive, I thought that having his favourite characters around him might make the transition from our flat a little easier.

He runs his fingers over the life-size characters, quoting some of the lines from the movie that we both know inside out, having watched it in excess of fifty million times. And that doesn't feel like an exaggeration.

Tonight will be our first night living here properly. I can't bring myself to move into the main bedroom – Mum's room – so I'm going to take my sister's old room. Which actually feels just as bad, so I'll probably end up sleeping on the sofa downstairs. But I couldn't put Ellis in either of those rooms. It felt wrong somehow to expect him to sleep where I won't. Plus, my old bedroom is the one he was used to sleeping in whenever he stayed over with Mum.

'Do you want to start unpacking your toys?' I ask, pointing to a cluster of cardboard boxes. 'You can arrange them on the shelves however you like.'

'My new bedroom is bigger than our whole old flat, Daddy,' Ellis says, still gazing up at his new wall art.

I laugh. 'It is pretty big.'

'And did it use to be yours when you were little, like me?' He drags his gaze away from the wall to look at me.

'It did.' I smile at his wondrous expression.

'I'm going to get my Scooby-Doo characters out first,' he says, rushing across the room to delve into one of the boxes. 'Oh, yes! My Sylvanian Family ponies!'

I leave Ellis to it for a while, although I know he'll probably get sidetracked and start playing with his toys rather than putting them away.

I wander next door into Mum's old room, a heavy feeling in my chest as I glance around the forlorn space. The bed is stripped, the wardrobes emptied – I finally found the emotional energy to pack up her clothes and take them to the charity shop. All her make-up, perfumes and toiletries are gone. I've kept some of her jewellery as a memento. None of it is valuable apart from her engagement ring, which I'll give to Ellis when he's older, in case he wants to get married.

If I do ever manage to fix up the house, it will be hard to redecorate Mum's bedroom. To paint over the walls and replace the furniture that's been here since we were kids. But the only alternative is to keep it as a shrine, like my sister's room. And that's not what my family would have wanted. They would have wanted Ellis and me to live our lives. To stamp our mark. But it's not easy to even think about this stuff, let alone actually do it.

I gaze out of the window into Mum's precious garden. At the dying flowers and shrubs, the grassy areas and pathways, the trees giving shade and privacy – evergreens dark and tall, the deciduous leaves turning all the colours of autumn. The veggie patch at the back, next to Dad's greenhouse. If we're able to stay here, I'll have to make the garden more low maintenance. I don't have the time or knowledge to look after a garden like this. Or maybe I'll learn.

With a practised eye, I know instantly what I could do to this home. An extension out the back to create a large family living area. Perhaps a balcony off this master bedroom. A side extension above the garage to add a fourth bedroom and en suite with dressing room. All the things I would have been able to do if Tamber had paid up. Or perhaps I wouldn't have. Perhaps I would keep the footprint the same and simply redecorate. After all, it's just the two of us here. Would Ellis and I need all that extra space? A house like that would need a bigger family to fill it.

I wonder if I'll ever meet anyone new. If I'll ever be able to trust anyone again after my ex left us. Part of me is happy to keep our family as just the two of us. A tight little unit. After all, it was me and Mum for years, and we did okay. But another side of me yearns to be part of a bigger family, like I had during my early years. What if I found a new partner and had more children? Brothers and sisters for Ellis. A tribe.

One of my fears is if something were to happen to me. Then Ellis would be left alone. What would happen to him? Perhaps his mother would step up and take him in. But would he be loved and cherished by her and her new husband? Or would he be treated differently to his half-siblings? The thought makes me panic. Maybe it's time I did think about looking for someone . . . although I have so many problems in my life right now that another complication is the last thing I need.

I sit on Mum's side of the bed, a wall of grief building up in my chest, like a tidal wave out of nowhere. I swallow it down, and swallow again, gritting my teeth against the loss. It would be a luxury to lie on the bed and cry. To let it all out. But I don't want to do that with Ellis in the next room. I need this to be a positive day for us. A new beginning. I'm going to order us a pizza and a box of cookies, even though money's tight. One treat can't hurt. A little boost to celebrate our new home.

As I get to my feet, I realise I never cleared out Mum's bedside drawer. I don't want to do it now, but I should probably just get it over with. I pause and then slide it open quickly before I have a chance to change my mind. I find her gold watch, some headache tablets, some loose change and a packet of tissues. I take the watch in my hand and remember it wrapped around her freckled wrist. It feels cold under my fingers. Mum gave me my stepdad's watch, but I refused to wear it after what he did. Or rather, what he didn't do.

Pulling the drawer out fully, I see a notebook right at the back. Mum always had various lists on the go – pieces of paper in her pockets or stuck to the fridge. Tasks that she'd cross off as she completed each one. She always tried to get me to do the same, but I prefer to keep things in my head. It would drive me mad to have bits of paper flying around all over the place. Perhaps Mum got herself this notebook to keep track of everything.

I place her watch back in the drawer and pick up the notebook. It's a hardback, lacquered in dark blue and worn at the edges. I'm suddenly nervous to open it, but I know I'm going to.

As I turn to the first page, I catch my breath, realising immediately what this is. I set it down on my lap for a moment, taking a few seconds to compose myself. To wonder if I have the strength to open it again.

Why the hell didn't Mum tell me about it? Why would she keep something like this a secret? My vision blurs and then refocuses as I reopen the book and flick through its lined pages, scanning the words. Horrified, yet devouring them hungrily. Until I come to a stop.

What?

NO.

But there it is, in black and white. The answer I didn't know I'd been seeking. I wrench my gaze from the page and stare straight ahead for a moment, my heart thundering in my chest. I can hardly believe what I've just read. It's worse than I ever could have imagined. I glance back down at the words, rage igniting deep in my body, so hot and red that I can barely see straight. I suddenly understand why Mum kept quiet about it. Why she hid this book away from me. It's because she was scared of what I might have done with the knowledge. And she was right. She should have got rid of it. She should have burned it.

This changes everything.

Chapter Thirteen

CHLOE

Nathan Blake:

Thanks to Abi for tracking me down and inviting me. I've managed to resist all social media until now!

Mark Steeples:

Mate, how are you doing? It's been years. You still in NZ?

Nathan Blake:

Yeah, but I'll be back in the UK in December for a few weeks. If I can change my ticket to a week earlier, I'll try to get to the reunion.

Abigail Matthews:

Be great to see you Nathan. So much to catch up on 😉 xx

Gareth Moore:

Nathan, mate. Hope you can make it.

My stomach flips as I devour Nathan's Facebook post, reading and rereading it, sipping my tea and allowing myself to get more than a little bit excited. I then go on to study his profile picture, clicking on it so it expands to fill the screen. He's wearing a dark T-shirt, looking directly into the camera, shading his eyes against the sun. His dark hair is unruly and he's clean-shaven, with a tan. Still as handsome as he was back at school. I click on his profile, but there are no friends shown aside from Abigail and Mark. No photos. No hint as to whether he's single, got kids. Nothing. But it looks like he only joined Facebook yesterday. Maybe he'll update his profile soon. Share a little more information about himself and what he's doing now.

Typical that Abigail's already flirting with him. Staking her claim with her winking emoji and those two kisses after her comment. If she was the one to track him down, they must have already messaged privately. I won't be embarrassing myself on Facebook. I'll wait until the reunion to talk to him in person. I keep refreshing the page to see if he's said anything else, but it's all maddeningly quiet in the group.

Anyway, I'd better stop – I feel like I'm turning into a stalker. Despite his apparent good looks, Nathan Blake might end up not being anything like I remember. He could be a total idiot these days. If he does end up making it to the reunion, I'll be pleased to see him, but I shouldn't pin my hopes on anything happening. I'm going there to reconnect with friends. To let my hair down for a change. Nothing more.

Even if the evening's a bust, at least it's nice to have something to look forward to. Half the fun of going anywhere is looking forward to it. The planning, deciding what to wear – all that. Although I've put on quite a bit of weight since my swimming days. I hope I'll be able to find something flattering. None of my good stuff fits me anymore. I'm guessing most people will be wearing designer outfits. I'll have to trawl through the TK Maxx racks to see if I can find something suitable.

My phone starts ringing in my hand and my mood plummets when I see that it's my mum video-calling. I really don't feel in the mood to deal with her usual barrage of negativity. But it keeps on ringing, plucking at my guilt. I should have put it on silent. I suppose I may as well answer; I have to let her know I'm coming back for the reunion anyway.

'Hey, Mum.'

'Chloe, I can't see you,' she cries. 'Is your camera switched on?'

'It's *your* camera, Mum. You have to tap it.'

After a couple of moments sorting out the technical stuff, my mum's face pops up on the screen. 'You look pale, Chloe. What's going on?'

'I'm fine, Mum.' The last thing I'm going to do is tell her about that threatening email and the stressful visit from Ben and his new family.

'Hmm,' she says, giving me one of her looks.

'What?'

'Got anything you want to say?' she asks, pursing her lips.

I know that particular expression of hers. She's cross about something. I'll try to distract her with the news that I've decided to attend the reunion. 'Well, there is actually—'

She carries on without waiting for a reply. 'Liz Trelawney came into our Tesco Express this afternoon, and told me you *are* going to the reunion after all!' Mum glowers through the screen. 'So when exactly were you planning on telling me this? Or weren't you?'

'Of course I was. I only made the decision recently.' Mum doesn't need to know that I've been planning to go for a while now.

'She said Jasmine mentioned it last week.'

'Well, last week is recently. I've been busy, Mum. Anyway, that's good news, isn't it? You wanted me to go to the reunion and now I'm going.'

'Hmm. Which weekend is it?'

'Next month. The last weekend in November. Would it be okay if I come back on the Thursday? I thought I might catch up with a few friends beforehand.'

'It's all right for some,' Mum grumbles, and gives a sniff. 'I don't want you coming in at all hours of the night. It's a small flat and I need my sleep.'

'I can book into a B&B if it's easier,' I reply through gritted teeth.

She starts fluffing out her hair, looking at herself on the screen rather than at me. 'Money to burn, have you?' she asks distractedly.

'You know I haven't. I'm just trying to fit in with your—'

'You can stay here, Chloe. It's not a problem. As long as you're respectful of me and the neighbours.'

'I'll be quiet as a mouse,' I reply.

Mum stops fiddling with her fringe and stares at me for any hint of mockery. 'Fine,' she eventually replies. 'Will you be out every night? Or will I get to see you some of the time?'

'Of course you'll see me. We can . . . I don't know, have lunch out one day, or something.'

'Money to burn,' she repeats knowingly.

I take a breath and try not to react. It's always been this way with Mum. Whatever I say is wrong. Whatever I do isn't good enough. You'd think I'd be used to it by now. As least she hasn't mentioned my ex-boyfriend Chris Tamber again. I saw his name pop up in the Facebook group and stayed well away in case I accidentally liked one of his comments.

'So, it's definitely okay for me to stay that weekend?' I ask.

She gives another sniff. 'You could Airbnb your flat while you're away. Some of those places charge a fortune.'

'Maybe.' I give what I hope is a placatory smile. 'So, is that a yes?'

'Yes,' she snaps. 'I already said yes. What do you want, a formal invitation?'

'Okay, Mum, thanks. Everything all right with you?'

She launches into a long tirade about how none of her staff know the meaning of a hard day's work. I let her get it out of her system, nodding and tutting in all the right places, but she can tell that I'm not really listening. I stifle a yawn.

'Am I boring you, Chloe?'

'No, of course not. Sorry, Mum, I'm just tired, I've been—'

'Fine, I won't keep you.' She reaches out to tap the screen.

'What? Mum, don't be like that.'

She stabs at the screen repeatedly, muttering that the damn thing won't turn off. Eventually, her face freezes as she ends the call.

I sigh, wondering if I should call her back. I feel terrible. I should have told her about my decision to attend the reunion before she heard it from Jasmine's mum, and I should have shown more interest in her work rant. She's just lonely. Like me, I guess. Heaven forbid I end up as miserable as her one day.

I scan the reunion group to see if there are any new comments, but there's nothing interesting so I check my other social media notifications – nothing there either. I'll check my emails before making something to eat.

I freeze at the sight of one of the email subject lines. I don't want to open it, but I can't seem to stop myself.

Stay at home

From: No Reunion

To: Chloe Flynn

You can block this email address too, if you like, but you better not show up at the reunion. Not if you know what's good for you.

Not again! My face heats up and my hands start shaking. I don't know if I'm scared or angry. Maybe both. With trembling fingers, I click on the sender's name. The email address is: noreunion2323@gmail.com – similar to the previous email, but with an extra 23 added. The letters blur before my eyes. I suppose if I block this address too, they'll just keep creating new accounts. I grit my teeth and take a breath, trying to calm my breathing. I'm not going to give them the satisfaction of replying, or blocking. I'm just going to mark it as 'spam' and ignore it.

My finger hovers over the spam button until my gaze snags on one of the lines:

Not if you know what's good for you.

I suddenly realise where I've heard that line before. Back when Ben and I were in the messy part of our break-up – the part where we were screaming and crying, hurling accusations at one another and realising that this was truly the bitter end – one of my best friends, Leila, came over to see me while Ben was at work. I'd thought she was popping round to commiserate with me, to be supportive, and I'd been so happy to see her. But it turned out that, of course, she was on Ben's side. They'd been friends for longer than Ben and I had been together, but Leila and I had become so close. I'd been a bridesmaid at her wedding. I'd been on a girls' holiday with her. We'd confided all our hopes and fears. So for her to turn her back on me when I'd needed a friend . . . it was such a slap in the face.

Anyway, she showed up on the doorstep, asking me to return a book she'd lent me a few weeks earlier. Said it had sentimental value and she didn't want me leaving without returning it. I'd asked what she meant about leaving. I told her I hoped the two of us would stay friends. That just because Ben and I were splitting up, that didn't mean we had to lose touch. She gave me such a cold stare, like I was something vile she'd stepped in. Told me that her loyalties lay with Ben and that I shouldn't start trying to turn people against him, *not if I knew what was good for me*. Her words really shook me up at the time. They felt like a threat. Like she would do something bad if I tried to hold on to my friendship circle.

Seeing that same line in this email feels like more than a coincidence. Could Leila be something to do with these threats? Maybe Wendi has roped her into it. Or Ben. But Ben has moved on with his life, hasn't he?

I can't connect the dots right now, but what if Leila's unhinged and is trying to ruin my life for some reason? I rack my brains to try to think of something I might have said or done to anger her, but I can't think of anything. She was always a bit wild, always the one who would do anything for a laugh – that was why people were drawn to her. But why would she go to such extremes? And why now? We had a great friendship; I know we did. But I remember the look on her face that last time I saw her. It wasn't the expression of a friend. It was the expression of someone who hated me.

Chapter Fourteen

My towel and swimming costume are gone. Despite the empty changing room, I try to cover my nakedness with my hands, rushing to my locker, my mind trying to make sense of my missing towel. Did I put it somewhere else? Did someone take it by mistake? But there's no one else here. It's just me – isn't it?

I glance around, but the changing room is empty. At my locker, I reach to open the padlock, only to realise that it's already open. I must have forgotten to lock it. Or . . . a terrible realisation has already begun to creep up my spine. The realisation that whoever took my towel and costume is the same person who managed to open my padlock. I unhook it and open my locker door, dread gnawing at my gut.

My schoolbag is inside, but my clothes are gone.

I glance up at the clock on the far wall. I'm supposed to be in my next lesson in eight minutes. It's Maths, and I'm scared of my teacher. She's unforgiving and doesn't accept any excuses for being late. My skin is chilly, but I'm suddenly hot with the panic and shame of not having my clothes. What am I going to do?

I root inside my bag in the vain hope there might be something I could wear, but there's nothing but books and my pencil case. I make my way along the bank of lockers, frantically testing each one to see if any are open, if I can just find a spare towel or some type of clothing, anything to cover my nakedness. Please let there be something. But they're all either locked or empty.

I swing around at the sound of a giggle, my heart thumping wildly, but there's no one here. No one I can see, anyway.

'Very funny,' I call out in a wavery voice. 'Can I have my towel back now?' I listen for a reply, but there's nothing. Maybe I imagined the laughter. But I know I didn't.

A large metal mop and bucket in the corner catches my eye. Maybe there's a cloth of some kind, a cleaning rag, anything. *I walk over to see that the bucket is full of liquid. Dirty water stinking of bleach that's been used to mop the floor. I wrinkle my nose. And then my heart drops as I spy my towel and swimming costume scrunched beneath the surface. I gingerly reach in to pull them out. They're dripping, ruined. Beneath them are yet more clothes. Before I've even pulled them out, I know they're mine. Everything has been dumped in here – my blazer, jumper, shirt, skirt, underwear. All soaking and stained with white patches of bleach.*

I haul my towel and clothing into the shower to rinse them all off, trying to squeeze out as much of the excess liquid as I can. The stench of bleach is overpowering, making my eyes water and my fingers sting. I suppose I should be grateful that they didn't leave me with nothing at all to wear. Wet clothes are better than no clothes. My white shirt is salvageable, but everything else is stained with pale splotches. Aside from the utter humiliation of having to walk out of here in soaking clothes, I'm dreading what Mum's going to say. She already baulked at the price of this second-hand uniform, so what's she going to say about forking out for another? What if she contacts the school and they conduct an investigation into what happened? That would be terrible. I'd be even more ostracised than I am now.

My throat burns with tears of impotent rage. I could weep, but I don't.

I won't give them the satisfaction.

Chapter Fifteen

CHLOE

I step off the train at Bournemouth station and wheel my case across the rain-slicked road to the bus terminal. Luckily, I don't have long to wait for the service to Poole Road where Mum lives in her little flat. The place where I grew up.

I could've taken a taxi, but it's rush hour so I'm hoping a bus might be faster. I get on and find a window seat halfway down the aisle, putting my handbag on the adjacent seat to discourage anyone from sitting next to me. The bus pulls out of the terminal with a hiss, and I find myself gazing through the steamy windows at familiar roads and landmarks. I notice a few new office blocks going up, as well as bars and restaurants that weren't around the last time I came back, and I realise guiltily that I haven't been here in months.

Being back in Bournemouth always conjures up strange emotions. Aside from recently reconnecting with Harriet and Jasmine, I haven't stayed in contact with anyone, so it feels quite lonely being here, as if my past has cut me out, moving on without me. Although my social life in Bath isn't exactly flourishing either. I pull myself up short, stopping my mind from veering down this path. I'm going out this evening with Harriet and Jas so I should be excited rather than melancholy. The three of us have kept in touch on WhatsApp over the past few weeks, messaging almost every day, so I'm sure we'll have a great time tonight.

Spying my stop up ahead, I press the bell, making my way down the aisle and heaving my case off the luggage rack. I thank the driver as the door whooshes open, letting in a blast of wind and a spattering of cold rain. Thankfully, I don't have far to walk. Mum's flat is only a hundred yards away from the stop.

I make my way along the wet concrete path towards the three-storey block made up of pale brown bricks and small white-framed windows. The only nod to design is the sharply sloping roofs of each wing. Arriving at the dark wooden front door, heavily pitted and scratched with age, I use my key to open it and bump my case over the threshold.

The entrance hall smells the same as it always has – stale dinners and air freshener. The common areas of my flat in Bath smell more welcomingly of freesias and furniture polish. I wrinkle my nose and grab the handle of my case. There's no lift, so I'll be hauling it up the two steep flights of stairs. I worry what Mum will do as she gets older, having to lug her shopping up the staircase. She won't want to move though; the flat is her sanctuary. She's spent years getting it just how she wants it. Her landlord lives abroad and is easy-going about how she decorates the place. As long as she pays her rent on time, he's happy.

'That you, Chloe?' Mum calls from her bedroom as I step into the pristine narrow hallway with its limewashed-framed prints of rustic Italian houses, Greek villas and French poppy fields. Mum's only been abroad once – to Portugal with a friend – and she hated it. *Too hot, no one spoke English, and you couldn't get a decent cup of tea anywhere.*

'Hi, Mum!'

She pokes her head out the door. 'You're late. Thought you'd be here an hour ago.'

'Didn't you get my text?' I say. 'The train at Southampton was delayed, and then the bus took for ever. You okay?'

'I'm due at work in half an hour. Just getting changed. Put the kettle on, will you? We'll have time for a quick cuppa before I go.'

I nod, leave my case in the hall for now and head to the kitchen, where I fill the kettle and try not to let this sudden creeping anxious feeling take over. I always get it when I come back home. The feeling that I'm not good enough. That I'm not capable of . . . *life*. That everything is just too much, too overwhelming.

Mum bustles out of her bedroom, dressed in her work uniform, just as I'm bringing our mugs into the lounge.

I stop dead, swallow and compose myself as I take in the new – and surprising – decor. 'This looks nice, Mum.'

She takes her tea from me, her cheeks turning pink at the compliment. 'I've gone for a Moroccan theme. I did it over the summer when I took my annual leave.'

'You never told me. You should've sent photos.'

She tuts. 'Photos never do things justice. Better to see it in real life. I painted the walls this terracotta colour and did some trellis stencilling. Then I picked up these rugs and brass lamps at a car boot sale. They came out of a Turkish restaurant in Charminster. The floral sofa spoils it a bit, but I think those velour throws give it a luxurious feel.'

'Looks lovely, Mum.' I make my way over to the sofa and gingerly perch between two oversized fringed and beaded cushions. 'How long are you working tonight?'

She sits in her favourite spot opposite the TV. 'Six-hour shift, so I won't be back till after midnight. You're off out, aren't you?'

'Yeah. I'm meeting up with Harriet and Jas in town.'

Mum sniffs. 'Jas Trelawney? Liz's girl?'

'Yeah.'

'She's a bit stuck-up, that one. Spoilt. Seem to remember fish fingers weren't good enough for her.'

'She's not stuck-up, Mum. She's vegetarian.'

Mum takes a sip of her tea and makes a face as though there's something wrong with it. 'Hmm, well, I hope you'll be able to make some time for me while you're down here. Or will you be out gallivanting the whole time?'

'Course we'll spend time together, Mum. I'll take you out for lunch tomorrow, okay?' I try to catch her eye. 'Unless you're working?'

'No – after tonight, I'm off till Sunday evening.'

'Perfect.' I give her a smile, hoping she'll return it.

Mum scowls down at her mug. 'Just going to put some more milk in this.' She gets up and leaves the room.

I try not to take her fault-finding personally. My mother has always been prickly; it doesn't mean she doesn't love me. It's just . . . I wish we got on better. All my old friends in Bath used to have enviable mother–daughter relationships. They would meet for coffee and lunches, have spa days. They were more like best friends. I shift in my seat, trying to get comfortable as I wonder where Mum and I went wrong. Maybe this visit will be the time we turn it around and become closer. I resolve to make an extra-special effort tomorrow. To talk about the things she loves. To listen. To not get annoyed by her disapproval or irritated by her moaning. I'll be the perfect daughter.

After Mum has left for work, I rinse our mugs and fetch my case from the hall, carrying it through to my childhood bedroom and dumping it at the foot of the single bed. Mum redecorated the room as soon as I left home. I was upset at the time, but I guess I understand. It's a small flat, and she needed the space. Gone were my posters and swimming trophies, my books and old CDs.

She packed everything up into cardboard boxes and left me a voice message instructing me to collect it all up that same month or it was going to the dump. Those boxes are now sitting untouched in a storage container in Bath, along with the other bits and pieces I boxed up after my divorce. I'm not sure why I'm hanging on to any of it. I'm probably never going to want to look at that stuff again. I should probably dump the lot.

My tiny childhood bedroom is now a shabby-chic fever dream with white-painted floorboards, rugs, distressed furniture, crystal-and-gold light fittings and cream fleur-de-lys soft furnishings. Unrecognisable from the teenage den it used to be.

I stare through the window on to the busy main road. Car headlights blur and haze in the rain. How many hours must I have spent gazing out of this window, wishing for a different life? But I'm not going to think like that anymore. From now on, I'm going to make the most of the life I have.

◆ ◆ ◆

Two hours later, I'm sitting at a table in Bar Thirty sipping espresso martinis with Harriet and Jasmine. Thursday is obviously the new Friday because the place is rammed.

'It's so great to have you here,' Jas says, her dark eyes crinkling, voice raised so I can hear her over the thumping bassline. 'Can you believe we haven't seen each other for fifteen years?'

'I know. Crazy, isn't it? Almost half our lives. You're married, I'm divorced.' I pull a face.

'Got your eye on anyone new?' Harriet asks.

'Chris is going tomorrow night,' Jas adds with a sly wink.

'Ugh, no thank you,' I reply. 'Been there, done that.'

They both laugh at my disgusted expression.

'How about you, Harrie?' I ask.

She tilts her head shyly and presses her lips together.

'Okay, spill, Miss Walsh,' Jas says, her face lighting up. 'Who is it?'

'No one,' Harriet replies unconvincingly. 'It's early days. I don't want to jinx it.'

'Um, not good enough,' Jas insists. 'I want a name. Details. Now that I'm a married woman, I'm living vicariously through both of you.'

Harriet laughs. 'How about I tell you if it turns into anything serious?'

'Spoilsport.' Jas gives her a mock glare, tossing a lock of shiny black hair behind her shoulder and turning her attention on me. 'So, Chloe . . .'

They're both staring at me now with curious grins on their faces.

'Don't look at me,' I say, feeling warmth creep up my neck. 'I've been single as a Pringle for months.'

'Okay, but who do you fancy?' Jas presses. My cheeks flame and Jas points at me triumphantly. 'I knew it! Tell us his name.'

'It's embarrassing,' I say, shifting in my seat and taking a few nervous gulps of my drink. Surely I'm not going to confess my teenage crush to them. I feel like I'm sixteen all over again.

'Of course it's embarrassing,' Jas replies. 'That's the whole point. Putting yourself out there. Making a fool of yourself. I love that part the best. I made a total dick of myself over Ash.'

'That's true.' Harriet nods and they both burst out laughing.

'But we'll talk about my love life another time,' Jas says. 'Right now, we need to know who *you're* making a dick of yourself over.'

'Well, I haven't done anything embarrassing yet, but maybe tomorrow . . .'

Harriet's mouth drops open. 'Someone from school? It *is* Chris!'

'I swear it isn't.' I finish my drink and sit back in my seat. 'Okay, promise you won't laugh . . . but I've always had the biggest crush on Nathan Blake.'

Instead of mocking me, they both nod sagely.

'Oh, yes,' Jas agrees. 'He's hot.'

'That boy is fire,' Harriet adds. 'Or at least he was, back in the day.'

I'm getting butterflies just thinking about him. 'I know, right, but what about Abigail? She's—'

'Abigail schmabigail,' Jas scoffs. 'No one in their right mind would go out with that drama queen.'

'Really? She's so pretty though,' I say, thinking of her glossy brown hair and blue eyes. 'And if her Facebook pictures are accurate, her figure's amazing too.'

'Um, have you seen you?' Jas says. 'You're like everybody's dream girl. You always got drooled over wherever you went.'

'I did not!' I protest. 'And if I did, that was years ago. These days, I'm a faded old hag.'

'Don't be ridiculous,' Jas snorts.

'Jas is right,' Harriet says. 'Blonde, curvy, big boobs, and you've got those cute dimples going on.'

I pull a face, knowing they're just being nice. These days, I'm on the heavy side and my natural hair colour is a boring ashy brown. It's only blonde because I splashed out on highlights last week.

'You're definitely going to make a move on Nathan tomorrow,' Jas insists. 'We'll be your wing woman, uh, wing women. Wow, that's a tongue-twister after a few drinks.'

'He might not even show up,' I say.

'I'm sure he will,' Harriet says, giving me an encouraging smile. 'Right, I'm going to the bar. Who wants what to drink?'

'Just a lemonade for me, please,' I reply. 'I need to take it easy tonight.'

'Yeah, to make sure you're on top form for Nathan tomorrow,' Jasmine teases with a wicked glint in her eyes.

I bat her arm with the back of my hand.

'Will your husband be coming along?' I ask.

Jas shakes her head. 'No, Ash would hate it. Plus, I'd have to look after him all night, make sure he wasn't bored. He only really knows Harrie.' Jas turns to Harriet and gives her shoulder a flick. 'What are you doing? You've been on your phone for ages. Thought you were getting the next round in.'

'Sorry, but look at this.' Harriet pulls a face. She passes me her phone, open at the reunion Facebook group. It shows Nathan's post from last month. Below it, Abi has commented again, offering him her spare room while he's in town.

Jas rolls her eyes. 'How obvious can you get?'

'At least he hasn't replied,' Harriet says, taking back her phone. 'Although . . .' She clicks on the screen and frowns. 'He has liked her comment. But that doesn't mean anything.'

I know it's stupid, but after seeing that comment, my good mood plummets. I bet the two of them will be an item before the reunion even starts. If I arrive and they're together . . . No. I need to stop being so negative. I told myself that tomorrow night is going to be the start of good things happening. I'm already enjoying myself way more tonight than I have in the whole of the past two years. If Abigail and Nathan do end up getting together tomorrow, then I'll forget about him and just have a good time with my friends, like I am this evening.

I clear my throat. 'Have you had any other messages about the reunion?' I ask, trying to keep it vague. I haven't told Harrie and Jas about the threatening emails in case they tell other people or make a big deal of it on the group page. The last thing I want is to be the centre of attention. That would be so awkward.

'Messages?' Jas frowns.

'Yeah, like people getting in touch privately, or . . . forget it. I don't know what I'm talking about.' I shake my head.

'No messages,' Harriet replies. 'Other than with you guys.' She smiles warmly.

'Just me then,' I mutter to myself. There have only been two horrible emails and I refuse to let some anonymous idiot intimidate me into staying away. In fact, they've made me more determined to attend. I'm going to show up tomorrow and make sure everybody sees me having a good time, especially the coward who sent them. They don't scare me. This isn't school and I'm not a kid anymore.

Chapter Sixteen

DEAN

Marilyn Parsons arrives at the house with one of her flowery biscuit tins. Recently, I've been trying to make sure Ellis eats more healthily as our diet has been getting a bit junk-food heavy. But I'll let it slide this once as I have other concerns on my mind tonight.

'Well, don't you look smart, Dean,' she says, looking me up and down, blinking. 'I hardly recognise you.'

I run a hand over my clean-shaven jaw. 'Thanks, Marilyn. Thought I'd better make an effort.' Tonight's event is black tie, which forced me to rent a suit for the occasion – money I could have done without spending. But at least it's for a good cause. *My* cause. 'It's really kind of you to babysit. I'm so grateful.' I welcome my neighbour into the hall.

'Nonsense!' Marilyn replies with a kind smile. 'You know how much I love that little lad. I don't see nearly enough of him. Speak of the devil.'

I glance up to see Ellis rushing down the stairs. 'Daddy, why are you wearing that funny tie? You look funny!' He giggles. 'Mrs Parsons, hello. Daddy said we could watch the Scooby-Doo movie, if we wanted.'

I'm so sorry, I mouth to her. 'You don't have to watch it if—'

'Oh, I love a good film,' she replies enthusiastically, patting my arm. 'Ellis, you'll have to tell me all about it. I haven't watched Scooby-Doo for years.'

I thank my lucky stars for Marilyn as Ellis slides his hand into hers and pulls her into the living room, chatting away about the characters and no doubt reaching for our battered copy of the DVD. We don't have any streaming services here. Just Mum's old Freeview box and her DVD player. I'm trying to keep my outgoings as low as possible. Thankfully, Ellis is still too young to be embarrassed or frustrated by our lack of current technology.

The two of us are quite settled in the house now. I still think of it as Mum's rather than ours, but that's okay; being here makes me feel closer to her. Of course, I have my down days, but keeping busy helps. I managed to let the flat to a young couple in their twenties. They were really happy to get it as they have a cat, and most rentals don't allow pets. I'd love to get a cat or a dog for Ellis once I know for certain where we're going to be living permanently. I guess it also depends on my work situation. At the moment, I'm labouring on building sites, keeping my head down until I sort out the Tamber nightmare. It's back-breaking, knackering work, but at least it gives me a chance to earn enough money for our day-to-day needs. And I can be home in time to pick Ellis up from after-school club.

I follow Ellis and Marilyn into the lounge, where the TV has already been switched on and the DVD inserted, ready for the Scooby-Doo bonanza that Ellis has planned for them.

'I've left you a choice of ready meals in the fridge,' I say to Marilyn. 'I think there's a lasagne and a shepherd's pie. But help yourself to whatever you like. Tea, coffee, all that stuff. Ellis has already had his tea, but he'll probably want a bowl of cereal before bed. Nothing too sugary, Ellis, okay?'

Ellis leans over and whispers something in Marilyn's ear.

She chuckles and tells him, 'We'll see.' She looks up at me with laughter in her eyes. 'Don't worry, Ellis and I will be fine,' she replies, waving me off. 'I hate to ruin your no-sugar rule, Dean, but I've got chocolate cake in my tin. I'll make sure he only has a very small slice. Off you go and have fun, and we'll do the same.'

'Okay, thank you,' I reply, wishing that I was indeed going out to have fun. Tragically, I can't even remember the meaning of the word.

It's been six weeks since I found the notebook in Mum's bedside drawer. During that time, I've been busy doing some digging. Every time I think of what was written there, my blood pressure shoots through the roof. I feel so frustrated. So utterly impotent. To know that it's too late to do anything meaningful to fix it. I'd give anything to be able to wind back the years. To have stopped it all from happening. But if I can't do that, then maybe I can do the next best thing.

'You've got my mobile number?' I check with Marilyn.

'Yes, I have. It's in my phone.' She pats her handbag.

'Great. All the emergency numbers are on the fridge – doctor, dentist, et cetera.'

'Dean, I promise we'll be fine.'

'Yes, I know. I . . . I'm not sure what time I'll be home.' A chill sweeps across my shoulders and, for the first time, I wonder if I'm doing the right thing. If maybe I should just stay home and forget all of it. Carry on with my life as it is. Burn the notebook, like Mum should have done.

But an image of Tamber's smug face flashes into my mind and I know I'll never be able to let this rest. To do nothing while that man walks around as though he owns the world and everything in it. As though he's some divine being instead of the low-life, bullying criminal he really is.

'Stay out as long as you like,' Marilyn urges. 'I'll be fine. I'm a night owl.'

'Okay, well, you're welcome to stay over if you get tired. There's bedding in the airing cupboard upstairs. The sofa's quite comfy, or there's Mum's old room . . .'

'Go. We're peachy, aren't we, Ellis?'

'Peachy?' Ellis dissolves into giggles.

I sweep up my son into a bear hug and kiss the top of his head, inhaling the warm, clean scent of shampoo, but he's already wriggling to be out of my arms. 'Bye, Daddy, have a nice time at your party. Put me down! It's starting! I have to sit with Mrs Parsons and tell her who everybody is.'

She pats the sofa and I watch my son snuggle into our neighbour's side. If anything should happen to me, I've specified in my will that I would like Marilyn Parsons to get custody of Ellis. I'm ninety-nine per cent sure that his mother won't object.

I glance at my watch as I leave the lounge and head towards the front door. West Cliff School reunion is due to start soon, but I'm not planning on arriving until a bit later. I want to slip in unnoticed. Keep my head down for a while until I get the lie of the land. Until I spot Chris Tamber.

Chapter Seventeen

CHLOE

'What do you think?' I step into the lounge, waiting for Mum's opinion on my outfit for tonight, preparing myself for the inevitable criticisms but hoping, for once, that she might say something complimentary.

Mum pauses the reality TV show she's watching and looks up at me. 'Very nice.'

I exhale and smile. 'Thanks, Mum!'

And then her eyes narrow. 'Isn't that dress a bit tight for you? It's very short, Chloe. You don't think it's a bit tarty for such a posh do? You might want to show a bit more class, seeing as it's at your old school.' She sucks air in through her teeth. 'Maybe a black dress rather than blue? You used to have a nice black dress when you were younger, but maybe it doesn't fit you anymore. You're not going to break your ankle in those heels, are you?'

Every word she utters robs a little more of my confidence, but I'm determined not to let her disapproval make me doubt how good I feel. Yes, the dress is tight, but it's fitted, not clingy. And it's definitely not tarty. It might be a bit short, but the neckline's not too low. It's tasteful. And even if it wasn't – *so what*? I can wear what I want.

'Glad you like it, Mum,' I reply, choosing to focus on her first sentence.

She purses her lips. 'Yes, well, I bet that cost an arm and a leg.'

'I got it in a charity shop for fifteen quid,' I reply smugly. 'I think it's a designer label, too.'

'I hope you got it cleaned. You can catch all sorts from second-hand clothes.'

'It's clean. Don't worry, Mum.' I won't tell her that the dry cleaning was double the price of the dress.

'It's my job to worry,' she says. 'You'll find out about that when you have kids of your own. *If* you have kids.' Her shoulders droop. 'I'd love grandchildren. You're already in your thirties and—'

'Okay, Mum, well, I'd better get going. Don't want to miss the next bus.' I feel bad for cutting her off, but a lecture on how I'm not getting any younger is not what I had planned for this evening. I make my exit, with promises to keep the noise down when I come in later. What does she think I'm going to do? Charge around with a herd of trumpeting elephants, yelling my head off?

My resolution to use this weekend to improve our mother–daughter bond has been a spectacular failure so far. Lunch today was at best uncomfortable, and at worst a disaster. I booked us a table at a really nice restaurant in Bournemouth Gardens, but Mum took one look at the menu and had a conniption about how over-priced everything was, and how the food at the local carvery was half the price and probably ten times better. I asked if she'd prefer us to go there instead, but she muttered something about how we were here now and that it would be rude to leave.

I tried to get her to open up about her life, to chat about her friends, about the other people at work. I complimented her on her interior design skills. But nothing I said elicited any joy or warmth. It was all negative. All misery. I wonder if she's always been this way, or whether she became bitter after my dad went off to start his new life, leaving her to raise me alone. I guess it's understandable that she's a bit resentful. She's her own worst enemy though. She complains about not having proper close friends, but I'm sure that's because she pushes them away with her negative attitude. I get that things have been tough for her, but why does she have to take it out on me? It's frustrating that we can't be closer. That I can't talk to her openly without her constant disapproval.

I'm reluctant to make an issue of Mum's attitude in case she takes it the wrong way; I'm scared of ruining what fragile connection we do have. I think I'll have to make peace with the fact that this is the nature of our relationship. And it's not going to change any time soon. Another unspoken fear swimming around my gut is that Mum doesn't want me to be happy. That she's purposely sabotaging my self-esteem because she's somehow jealous of my life. But whenever the tendrils of those kinds of thoughts begin to curl around my brain, I always uproot them straightaway. No one wants to believe that of their own mother.

Outside the flat, despite the traffic fumes and the damp, blowy weather, I can finally breathe again. Banishing thoughts of my mother from my mind, I focus on the evening ahead. I decided not to let the anonymous emails put me off attending, or stop me looking forward to tonight. I realise it was ridiculous to think that it could have been my old friend Leila who sent the messages. Other than her loyalty to Ben, what other reason could she possibly have to want me to stay away from my school reunion? For that matter, how would she even know about it? No, chances are it's some bitchy classmate who never grew up. My money would be on Abigail Matthews, and I would never give her the satisfaction of seeing me scared, even if there's still an annoyingly persistent pulse of fear behind my ribcage. I'm sure it will fade once I get to the venue.

My bus is already trundling down the road towards my stop so I clutch my jacket tighter around me and totter along the pavement to flag it down, relieved when it pulls over before I've reached the stop. I hop on, say hi, tap my card and choose a seat near the front, nervous excitement making my skin tingle. It's less than a five-minute journey to Westbourne, but the walk would have taken fifteen minutes and it's already started to spit rain. A storm is forecast for later and I don't want to ruin my freshly waved hair or my outfit. Plus, I can't walk far in these heels. I'm meeting Jas and Harriet for a drink beforehand in a swanky new bar, The Lucky Rabbit, as I don't have the courage to turn up to the reunion on my own.

I take a few deep, calming breaths, telling myself to be confident and to have fun. To not dwell on past hurts. I'm a grown woman with a life of my own. I don't need anyone else's approval. I'm no longer a kid. I'm not that teenager anymore. I jump as my phone buzzes in my lap. Ignoring the anxious flutters in my belly, I tap the screen and the email opens:

> Stay at home
>
> From: No Reunion
>
> To: Chloe Flynn
>
> I hope you're tucked up in bed, Chlo. No one wants to see you at the reunion tonight. Least of all me.

My vision blurs as I scan the words. Try to make sense of them. I tell myself it was predictable that they'd message me on the night of the reunion. Of course they would. But that doesn't make me feel any less shaken up.

Chlo? They called me *Chlo*! There's only one person who used to call me that – Chris Tamber. I know he was upset with me back then, but what did he expect, after everything? I glance up suddenly, worried I might have missed my stop, but as I squint through the huge windscreen, it looms into view. I stand on wobbly legs and press the bell, gritting my teeth in anger and shock, the backs of my eyes stinging with tears. If Chris is there tonight, I'll . . .

The bus lurches to a stop and I almost fall, clutching at the railings on the luggage rack to steady myself.

'You all right, love?' the driver asks.

'Fine, thanks,' I reply in a strangled voice.

The door whooshes open and I step out into the rain and head towards the wine bar in a discomfited daze. I need to get back into the positive, confident frame of mind I had before that email arrived. I can't let them get into my head like this. Whoever it is knows what they're doing. If their aim is to unsettle me, it's working.

It's only six thirty so the place isn't too busy yet. I spot my friends straightaway, standing at the bar. They wave me over, big grins on their faces. I try to match their smiles with one of my own, but it takes all my effort to keep it there. I feel like crying, not partying.

'You look amazing, Chloe!' Harriet says.

'Gorgeous!' Jas adds. 'Loving the colour of your dress! The blue matches your eyes.'

Their compliments lift my spirits a little, and boost my confidence after Mum's damp reaction to my outfit.

'Thanks,' I reply, looking them up and down admiringly, pushing the hateful email from my mind. 'But what about you two hotties?!'

Harriet's wearing an emerald-green sequinned cocktail dress, and her light-brown hair has been pulled back into a sleek chignon.

Jasmine looks stunning in a three-quarter-length, off-the-shoulder red silk dress with a side-split up to her thigh. Her dark hair hangs in a curtain down her back.

'We've ordered a bottle of Veuve Clicquot and three glasses,' Harriet says. 'You in?'

'Sounds good to me,' I reply, slipping off my jacket and draping it over my arm. I haven't experienced this kind of nervous energy for years.

We stay at the bar, perching on stools and chatting to a flirty barman who's way younger than us. By the time we've polished off the bottle of champagne, it's almost seven o'clock.

'The taxi should be here any minute,' Harriet says.

'Get ready for *Operation Chloe and Nathan*,' Jas declares.

'Don't do anything embarrassing!' I beg, my pulse suddenly thrumming with anxiety at the thought of possibly humiliating myself in front of all my old classmates. I also can't help my thoughts returning to who might have sent those threatening emails. And what they might do when they see that I've ignored their warning to stay away.

Chapter Eighteen

CHLOE

The taxi pulls up on to the sweeping driveway. I'm in the front seat and Jas and Harriet are in the back. Three has always been an awkward number, and I couldn't help feeling a little left out on the short journey over, hearing them chatter away in the back while I made small talk with the taxi driver – a woman in her late forties with four kids, who wanted to hear all about tonight's reunion. But it's silly to be jealous; after all, I've excluded myself from their friendship for years.

I'm not sure what I was expecting, but West Cliff School looks almost exactly the same as it did fifteen years ago, its stone facade floodlit like a castle in a fairy tale. Ridiculously grand and impressive; from the outside, at any rate. We pay the driver and exit the cab, dashing for the entrance, hands over our heads, trying to dodge another icy rain shower.

Inside the foyer, I hear Katy Perry being played over the sound system and I'm hit by a sudden wave of memories. Flashbacks to a school disco where Mum only let me stay till 10 p.m. instead of midnight, to being jostled on the stairs by the older kids, to arriving late for a lesson and being told off in front of everyone. Normal school memories, I suppose, but unsettling nevertheless. That feeling of never really belonging. The gut-twisting fear of drawing negative attention from the popular kids, of not having quite the right hair-style, the right shoes, the right bag, worrying about the standard of my work, obsessing about the terms of my scholarship – to keep performing at a certain level to stay in the swim academy. All these emotions roar at me like a tidal wave breaking so fast I can barely breathe.

But I keep moving along with Harriet and Jas, pretending that I'm okay, picking out my name badge, agreeing that everything is wonderful and exciting and that we're going to have such a great night. I knew it would feel strange to be back here, but I hadn't expected such a visceral reaction to the place.

'Just going to the loo,' I say in a breezy voice that covers my inner turmoil, pointing to a door down the corridor. I just need a moment or two to get a grip on my emotions before I go into the hall. To get back to the fun, happy person I was at the bar earlier. I can't let tonight slip by as another opportunity that I ruined for myself.

'Good idea,' Jas replies. 'I need to sort my face out before we go in.'

The three of us file through the door. It's been revamped since our day. Now it's all individual cubicles with their own mirrors and washbasins, rather than the communal area we used to have where cliques of girls would hang out and terrorise the weaker pupils at lunch and break times. I go into one of the cubicles and lock the door, stare at my ghostlike reflection in the mirror, patting my face to bring the colour back. I don't look like me.

Giving myself an internal pep talk, I think about who I am now, not who I was then. I'm a confident person. I look okay. I have a job, my own apartment. I'm here with two lovely friends. Everything is great. And maybe I'll even get a chance to speak to a boy I used to have a crush on. There's nothing to worry about.

Nothing can touch me here. I breathe deeply, feeling the panic subside. Coming back to normality again. With faintly trembling fingers, I reapply my lip gloss and rake my fingers through my newly blonde waves. It's just a bit of the jitters, that's all. Quite normal and nothing to stress about.

Over the next half hour, everything is a blur of squeals and hugs as we bump into old friends. The school hall has been decorated with balloons, fairy lights and streamers, and a banner has been strung above the stage proclaiming this to be the *CLASS OF 2008*.

The three of us make a beeline for the bar, where we knock back a couple of flaming Drambuies – for old times' sake – then buy a bottle of Prosecco to take to our table. It's comforting to have Jasmine and Harriet by my side. It would have felt far more intimidating to have arrived here on my own.

Most people are instantly recognisable, just more groomed and polished than back at school, although I guess this is a reunion party so everyone's dressed to impress – including me. Over the past fifteen years, the men have broadened out, and the women seem more confident. Of course, there are a few more laughter lines, and the occasional sprinkling of grey hair. I've already studied my classmates' profile pics and photographs online, but it's not quite the same as seeing them here in the flesh. It's weird us being back in this place where we spent so many years, now all grown up, chatting as adults. It almost feels as though we're kids pretending.

I don't know what I was expecting, but I can't get over how friendly everyone seems. There's none of the bitchiness and whispering like there was at school. Just open smiles and warm hugs. Although I haven't been here for long, so I guess there's plenty of time for people to show their true colours. Unless . . . maybe everyone truly has grown up. Everyone apart from my anonymous emailer. I push them from my mind and try to concentrate on having a good time.

'Oh my GOODNESS, Chloe Flynn!' A girl heads over to our table. Her voice is ultra-posh, and she's wearing a long black sparkly dress that looks like it cost thousands. 'It is you, isn't it?' she asks, staring hard at me and then nodding as she spots my name tag. 'You look amazing. That dress is incredible on you.'

I give her a smile, panicking slightly as I don't recognise her face and I can't spot a name tag. 'Oh . . . thank you.'

'It's me, *Georgia*. Georgia Cavendish. You were in my English, and Biology.' Her eyes narrow slightly.

I smile. 'Of course, Georgia, hi, sorry.' I remember her now. I think we probably spoke three times at the most during my five years at West Cliff. She's the girl whose party I went to in Year 7. 'You arranged the reunion, didn't you?' I'm trying to match her face with her Facebook profile picture, suddenly remembering that it's a photo of her pouting in a bikini and sunglasses on a yacht.

'I did arrange it, yes,' she gushes. 'I do a bit of events organising these days – beach polo, charity dinners, that kind of thing. I'm honestly so thrilled you could make it. There's a raffle later, make sure you buy some tickets. And we'll have to have a proper catch-up.'

I'm a little thrown by her friendliness, but it's also quite flattering. 'That would be—'

'Oh my goodness, *Marcus*!' Her attention is taken by Marcus Lee, who's sitting at the next table with his wife and another couple I don't recognise. Marcus used to be in the rowing academy. I think I heard he's now a newly elected member of parliament. Georgia pats my shoulder. 'Darling, we'll absolutely have to have that catch-up later.' With that, she blows me a kiss and sashays over to Marcus's table.

I shrug at Jasmine, who rolls her eyes. 'What's the betting that catch-up never happens?' she asks.

'Oh, daaahling, don't be such a cynic,' Harriet replies.

'She certainly knows how to work her way round a room,' I say, watching her fawn over Marcus.

Jasmine nudges me and angles her head at a table on the opposite side of the dance floor. Sitting there are three girls I instantly recognise – Abigail Matthews, Zara Wickes and Gemma Radcliffe. The queens of our year. A cluster of guys has gathered around their table and my stomach lurches as I spy my ex-boyfriend, Chris Tamber, among them. The one who taunted me for four years until he decided I was pretty enough to go out with. The one who I'm fairly sure has been sending me those horrible emails. Nerves claw at my insides. I turn away, worried he'll see me looking. The last thing I want is to attract his attention. Not until I'm ready to confront him.

'I love this song!' Jas squeals, jumping up from her chair as Amy Winehouse's 'Valerie' starts playing. She holds out her hands to me and Harriet. 'Come and dance.'

I glance at the empty dance floor. 'Maybe later,' I reply. There's no way I'm getting up there in front of everyone right now. In front of *him*. I'm going to need a few more drinks and a bigger crowd to hide behind before I brave a dance.

'Harrie?' Jas pleads, her dark eyes widening, her lower lip jutting out.

Harriet shakes her head. 'I'm with Chloe on this.'

'Come on, Chloe.' Jas isn't giving up. She takes my hand and tries to pull me off my chair.

'I said, later!' I snap.

Jas lets go of my hand, a startled expression on her face.

I'm instantly contrite. 'Sorry, Jas. I'm just . . . I'm not as confident as you.'

Harriet glances at Jas and then turns back to me, her lips pressed together.

I realise they're both a bit shocked by my outburst. I try to explain. 'I'm just a bit nervous about seeing everyone this evening. Honestly, the thought of them all staring at me on the dance floor . . . I didn't mean to snap. Sorry.'

'Don't worry about it,' Jas says.

'Look . . .' Harriet points across the dance floor. 'Abi and her coven are going for it. You could dance with them, Jas.'

'Very funny,' Jas replies, and plonks herself back down in her seat.

Harriet catches my eye and grins. I'm relieved they've forgiven me. But the smile is wiped from my face as I see who's started walking across the dance floor in my direction.

It's Chris.

I guess there's no avoiding him. I knew I'd have to speak to the man. Might as well get it over with. Now that I'm faced with Chris in person, I'm having doubts about him being the one behind the emails. And even if it was him, do I want to have an argument here, now, in front of everyone? Jasmine unsubtly nudges Harrie and they move away. I want to tell them to stay, but my mouth has gone dry.

My hands are sweaty and my mind is racing. I remember the last time I spoke to Chris Tamber. Please, God, don't let him bring any of that up tonight. I need that to be over and done with. If we can have a normal mundane conversation right now, then maybe I'll finally be able to put all of that history behind me and move on.

'Hey, Chlo. It's been a while,' Chris says softly, leaning in for a kiss on the cheek that's far too close to my mouth. The familiar expensive scent of him sends a bolt of panic through me. He's still handsome. Still fit. Still arrogant.

'Hi,' is all I can manage for the moment, my mind a strange mix of numb and frantic.

'I was hoping you'd come tonight,' he says, his voice deep and confident. 'You look incredible.'

Annoyingly, I feel myself blush. 'To be fair, everyone looks incredible tonight,' I reply, trying to make light of his comment.

'You never could take a compliment, Chlo.'

I shrug. 'Are you sure you wanted me to come here tonight?' I ask. 'Maybe you'd have preferred it if I'd stayed away?' I examine his face for signs that he knows what I'm referring to. For a clue that he's the one behind the emails.

'Stayed away?' His forehead wrinkles. 'Why would I want that?'

I can't tell if he's truly baffled by my question or if he's a good actor.

'What are you doing these days?' he asks casually. 'You moved to Bath, right?'

I nod, wondering how he knows that. Maybe I mentioned it on Facebook. I don't think I did though. 'I'm in banking now,' I reply. He doesn't need to know the ins and outs of my job. Not that it matters what I do, but these people have always made me feel insecure about my background. Especially Chris bloody Tamber, who owns half the county.

'Nice.' Chris nods.

'How about you?' I ask politely, to keep him talking about mundane things while I figure out how I should play this.

'Oh, you know, I went into the family business,' he replies.

'Great.' I drain my glass of Prosecco, turning to pour myself another, but I see Jasmine has taken the bottle with her.

'Can I get you another drink?' Chris asks, noting my empty glass.

I hate that he's being so attentive. 'No, thanks. I'm taking it easy tonight,' I lie. 'Don't want to get too drunk and make an idiot of myself.'

'Yeah.' He smiles lazily. 'You wouldn't want to see yourself plastered all over our Facebook group in compromising positions.'

My chest tightens.

'No husband?' he asks unsubtly. 'Boyfriend?'

'I'm divorced.' I manage to choke out the words, wishing more than anything that Ben was by my side right now, if only to deter Chris. Perhaps I should have lied and told him I was still married.

'His loss,' he says with a sympathetic smile.

'I heard you got married,' I say. 'Congratulations.'

'We're separated,' he replies with a rueful smile. 'Pretty sure she's currently off in her lair planning how much she can screw out of me in the divorce.'

'Sorry to hear that.' I give what I hope is a sincere frown.

'*Are* you?' He raises an eyebrow, trying to flirt.

I can't deal with this right now. With *him*. It's too much. I need to shut this down asap. I turn and mouth *help* to Jas and Harrie, who are chatting with some guys on another table. Bless them, they come straight over and start quizzing Chris about school while I duck out of the conversation and head back to the bar to get myself something stronger to drink. I don't think Chris is going to be deterred tonight. He's still talking to my friends, but I notice from the corner of my eye that his attention is laser-focused on me. Whether because he's interested in me romantically or there's something more sinister on his mind, I don't know. Either way, I decide to steer well clear. I didn't come here tonight to deal with Chris. I came to have fun. To kick-start my stalled life.

I wrench my thoughts from Tamber and glance around the hall, searching. Hoping that Nathan might have shown up. But he's not here. Even though I told myself not to get hung up on him, disappointment fills my chest. I don't think he's coming.

Chapter Nineteen

As I sit on the bench at the side of the pool, I see him smirking at me from the viewing gallery. It's not a cruel smirk either. I would expect that. No. It's a flirty smirk, accompanied by a gaze that rakes over my body. I look away, ignoring the laughter that comes from his section of the gallery, hoping I'm too far away for him to see my discomfort at their scrutiny of me in my swimsuit. I hunch over, feeling exposed.

My race is coming up next and the whole year is here to witness it. There are decades of competitive history between the six schools competing here today. West Cliff takes winning very seriously. But it's fine. I know I can do it. I'm more nervous about tripping over my feet on the way to the starting blocks than I am about losing the race.

But why is Chris Tamber paying me so much attention? If he's started noticing me, then that's not good. To be on his radar is to bring down a world of pain upon my head. He's the richest, best-looking, most popular boy in school. His parents came here and so did his grandparents – the school library is called the Donald Tamber Library after his grandfather. His family has donated thousands. I wouldn't be surprised if they changed the name of the whole school to honour his family.

I daren't glance up again. I tell myself he's only looking at me because of the race. Because I'm the one in the spotlight. It's only natural that everybody from my school will have their eyes on me. Surely his gaze is nothing more than that. Surely he doesn't know my secret.

Against my better judgement, my eyes stray up to the gallery, where Chris is still staring at me without shame, his friends nudging him and making rude gestures. I look straight back down into my lap, telling myself that once the race is over, he'll go back to not knowing I exist. I'll make myself invisible. After all, aside from being the best at swimming, being invisible is my greatest desire.

Chapter Twenty

DEAN

After parking my van in the next road, I stride along the wide, dark street, breathing in cold, damp November air that billows up from the sea and over the clifftop. I'm thankful for the brief gap in the rain. Following the curving line of the coast, the roads in this part of Bournemouth are studded with lofty pine trees that shield grand homes set back from prying eyes. Victorian street lamps cast intermittent pools of light so that I alternately feel hidden and then suddenly exposed, even though there's no one around on such a dark, stormy evening.

Turning into the next road, I spot the entrance to the venue up ahead, flanked by two grey stone pillars. In front of a low stone wall, topped with a dense privet hedge, a dark green sign on two metal posts proclaims this to be West Cliff School.

I've arrived.

Pausing at the first pillar, I gather my nerve for the evening ahead. If I were a smoker, I'd be sucking down nicotine right now. I wish I had something to calm my jitters. I was tempted to bring a hip flask for a shot of Dutch courage, but decided against it. Far better to be clear-headed. A vague plan for tonight sloshes around my mind. I'd love to have sorted out something more concrete – a schedule for how I envisage things playing out – but there are too many variables, depending on how lucky I get. I've done as much forward planning as I could, but the rest will be down to chance.

Shoving my hands into my pockets, I make my way along the dark, winding driveway, loose concrete and gravel crunching beneath the soles of my polished shoes. I focus on the huge floodlit building up ahead, while trying to avoid potholes and puddles. A car's headlights startle me and I press into the trees to conceal myself while it cruises past, heading towards the school. I don't know if its occupants saw me. I pray they don't slow to try to get a closer look. But it's fine. They keep going and, now that I'm out of their headlights, I can merge back into the darkness.

I wonder again if this is a really bad idea. *What was I thinking?* If the sight of a car can unsettle me this much, then what will a hall full of people do? Tamber has that non-mol order against me. The hearing's next week. If this goes badly, chances are I'll end up in prison. Or worse. I step out from the trees once more. It's not too late to turn around. To hop back into my van and drive home to my boy. To stop this madness. But then what? Am I supposed to simply let Tamber get away with everything he's done to my family? Is that how the world works? Or do I do something? Attempt to get some sort of justice? I don't want to be the kind of person who backs off for an easy life.

I take my hands out of my pockets and blow on my fingers to try to warm them. My eyes are streaming in the cold air, my feet are numb. But despite my worries and my discomfort, I'm still resolved. *Of course I'm not going home.* Once the occupants of the taxi have entered the building, I continue making my way down the driveway, more determined than ever that I'm going to see this through to its conclusion. Whatever that might be.

West Cliff School is an imposing sight. Even more so to someone like me who attended an unflashy red-brick secondary school with blue-framed windows and suspended ceilings. A regular school that looked like a doctor's surgery or a community centre. This building before me is made of solid grey stone, four storeys high, with leaded sash windows, bays, turrets and crenellations, like something out of a fantasy movie. I can't imagine what it must have been like to go to school here.

A distant thump of music emanates from the building and a wash of laughter follows on the wind. The sooner I get in there, the sooner I can get this done. With renewed determination, I cross the half-moon-shaped forecourt and stride up the wide stone steps to the arched double doors banded with metal and studded with rivets like they belong to a castle rather than a school. A fortress designed to keep people out. People like me.

I needn't have worried. There's no security on the door. I push against it and it swings open silently. The reception hall is grand, with parquet floors, a crystal chandelier and a sweeping staircase that curves up and out of sight into darkness. The music is louder in here, echoing through the air and vibrating inside the walls. To my right, I see two women seated at a table next to a corridor. They wave and beckon me over and I try to act like I belong, injecting some swagger into my walk.

'Hello.' They grace me with bright smiles. 'Here for the reunion?' the dark-haired one asks. As though I'll be here for anything else, decked out as I am in my dinner jacket.

'Yeah,' I reply. 'Sorry I'm a bit late.'

'Don't worry, I'm sure it'll go on till the early hours. Lots of time to catch up with everyone.'

'Were you in my year?' I squint at the women as though trying to place them. They seem a bit older.

'Kind of you to say, but no, we're just helping out. Staying on reception until nine and then we'll lock up, let you all get on with it. You'll have to leave by the main hall exit after that.'

'Okay, no problem.' There are three remaining name tags on the table. I take one of them and pin it to my lapel while the dark-haired woman ticks me off on her list.

'Have fun,' they call after me.

I wave in reply, my palms sweating as I make my way along the corridor towards the sound of music and laughter. A set of double swing doors ahead look like they lead into the hall and the reunion party. The doors are made from heavy wood with wired-glass panels set into the top half. I peer through to see a typical set-up – a dark hall with flashing disco lights, a DJ on the stage, balloons, streamers, banners and other decorations. A temporary bar in the corner, a buffet running the length of one wall, and tables and chairs around the dance floor.

There must be at least a couple of hundred guests. Partners were invited so I'm guessing only half to two-thirds are ex-pupils, which makes it easier for me to blend in. I can't spot Tamber. He'd better be in there after all the trouble I've gone to getting here. Although if he's not, then I guess that will be that.

I push open the door to a wall of sound. Everyone's dressed to the nines. Most are either seated at the tables, queuing up for the buffet or clustered around the bar. Only four have made it on to the dance floor, jumping around to Kaiser Chiefs' 'Never Miss a Beat'.

I instantly break my vow and head to the bar, ordering two tequila shots and downing them one after the other. Then I order a pint of pale ale to sip while I get my bearings. I settle into a dark corner, leaning against a pillar as I scan the room.

Most of the men are dressed in black dinner jackets, same as me, and a few are wearing regular suits. I guess I could have got away with wearing my old suit after all, but this get-up allows me to blend in better. To look like I truly belong to this privileged group. My gaze suddenly lands on Tamber, his head thrown back in raucous laughter. Although he's the reason I came tonight, it's a shock to see him in the flesh again after our last unpleasant encounter. And, once again, I'm on his turf. In his world. At least tonight I can time things a bit better, and he won't be surrounded by security guards. Although he will be with all his friends.

He's standing with a group of around half a dozen men. They're all confident and wealthy-looking, flashy watches on their wrists, smart haircuts, broad-shouldered. Women flutter around them, vying for their attention. But Tamber's eye keeps straying over to a gorgeous blonde woman in a blue dress that clings to her curves in all the right places. She really is breathtaking, standing next to a table on the other side of the dance floor, talking to two other women who are seated. She's not giving Tamber any attention whatsoever. Either she hasn't noticed that he can't take his eyes off her, or she's ignoring him on purpose. I hope it's the latter.

Watching all this camaraderie going on around me, without me – friends catching up, reminiscing about their shared past – I feel as though I'm not really here. Like I'm watching a TV show rather than physically standing in this impressive hall with its panelled walls and vaulted ceiling. I've been planning this evening for so many weeks that I can hardly believe I actually made it this far. But I guess this is the easy part.

It's what comes next that's going to be the real test.

Chapter Twenty-One

CHLOE

Jasmine finally gets her way and coaxes me and Harrie on to the now crowded dance floor. We're joined by more people – some who I remember, and others I don't. Before long, we're all smiling, laughing, singing, leaping around. It feels like a release from the two years' worth of sadness I've had in my heart. I've been dragging my divorce around with me for so long that I'd forgotten how to enjoy myself.

It's cathartic to let go and have fun, dancing away to the songs from our teenage years. We know all the words, all the riffs; we remember all the dance moves we used to practise in our bedrooms. It's as if our grown-up cares have melted away and we've reverted to a time when a three-minute song could sum up everything we were feeling.

I've managed to avoid another encounter with Chris this evening, and I've accepted that Nathan Blake isn't coming tonight. That my desire to see him was probably nothing more than a symbol for my new start. Something to focus on, to get excited about. But, as the music pulses through me and I let go of my tightly held inhibitions, I realise I don't need a man to kick-start my life. I'm doing it all on my own.

The instant I have that realisation is the moment I spot him.

Is that him? I'm sure it is. My stomach flutters.

He's standing at the bar, laughing with friends. The music seems to fade for a moment. I lose my rhythm and stop dancing. Stand breathless on the crowded dance floor. I can't stop staring. He looks just like his profile pic, only more gorgeous, if that's possible, wearing a tux. Tall, broad-shouldered – a man rather than a boy – dark-haired and dark-eyed. I can't believe he's actually here.

I blink and carry on dancing, although now I'm detached from the music, my brain and heart both speeding out of time. I'm not confident enough to go over there and talk to him yet; I need time to compose myself. I'm a sweaty mess. And I'll also need a drink for courage. I think we have another half a bottle of Prosecco left. I weave my way back to the table, where I sit and pour myself a large glass, my hands trembling. I take a couple of gulps and slip my phone from my bag, opening the camera app to check my hair and touch up my make-up.

He's actually here.

All my daydreams are coming at me. All my wishes and hopes. My childish fantasies. I peer through the crowd until I spot him once more, but my hopes instantly disintegrate when I see who he's with. Abigail Matthews and Zara Wickes are all over him, flicking their hair, pushing out their chests and laughing obnoxiously. He looks as though he's enjoying the attention. I wonder if he took Abigail up on her offer to crash at her place. But surely, if that were the case, they would have arrived here together.

'Hey, Chlo.'

A deep voice cuts through my thoughts. I look up with a start to see Chris hovering over me again. My heart sinks. Can't he take the hint that I'm not interested? I want to concentrate on Nathan. On what I should do to get his attention without making it seem like I'm throwing myself at him. Basically, I need to do the opposite of what Abi and Zara are doing. But I won't be able to do anything with Chris hanging around. I can't even think straight while he's in my face like this.

'Hi,' I reply unenthusiastically, hoping he'll pick up on the vibe and leave me alone.

He sits in the chair next to mine and shifts it closer, blocking my view of Nathan.

Irritation and revulsion make me tense. The urge to get up and walk away is strong, but I don't want to make him feel angry or rejected. How can I get him to *want* to leave me alone? If he's behind the emails and truly didn't want me to come tonight, he's got a strange way of showing it. The best thing I can do is to forget those messages and treat Chris like anyone else, not let him see how shaken up I feel by his proximity.

'Having a good night so far?' he asks.

'Amazing,' I reply, managing to sound upbeat. 'I haven't danced this much in ages. My feet are killing me – in a good way.'

'I saw you out there enjoying yourself.'

I cringe inwardly at the thought of him watching me. 'Have you kept in touch with many people from school?' I ask, scraping my chair back to create more space between us, and to retrieve my view of Nathan, but I've lost sight of him.

'A few. Gareth, Marcus, Georgia, Abi, Zara . . . the usual lot. Not that I have much time to socialise these days. Too busy with work. How about you? I saw you come in with Harriet and Jasmine. You've stayed in contact?'

'Not really. We only reconnected this year,' I reply. 'Because of the reunion.'

'That's a long time to have lost touch. A lot of wasted years,' he adds, trying to catch my eye. Trying to make this into a meaningful 'moment'.

'It was great of Georgia to arrange tonight,' I say, attempting to lighten things up. To steer the conversation away from our past. 'Sounds like she's found her calling – a born party planner, that one.' I force out a grin.

'Fifteen years, Chlo,' he says softly, ignoring my attempt to change the subject.

'I know. It's a long time,' I reply.

'Don't you remember how good we were?' he persists. 'For the whole of Year 11 it was, *Chloe and Chris, Chris and Chloe* – we were inseparable.'

'I know, but before that you thought I was a dork.' I smile to let him know I'm not holding a grudge. 'Made my life a misery, you did.' I prod his chest with my forefinger.

He catches it and takes my hand. 'I was just a stupid kid. Didn't know any better.' He pins me with a look that makes me squirm. 'But I'd love to get to know you again, as an adult. If you'll let me.' These are not the words of someone who didn't want me here tonight.

I ease my hand from his grasp and wrap my arms around myself. 'I don't think that's a good idea. Too much history, you know? I need to move forward with my life, not backwards.' I'm talking to Chris, but I can't stop thinking of Nathan. I glance over Chris's shoulder to try to catch another glimpse. To see if he's still talking to Abigail and Zara, but there are too many people blocking my line of sight.

'You said you were in banking . . .'

His abrupt change of subject wrongfoots me. 'Um, yeah, boring, I know.'

'Not at all. I was wondering what type of banking? Who are your clients? I might be looking to move part of my business to somewhere new. Maybe we could meet up next week to discuss possibilities?'

If only he knew how lowly my position actually is. The sort of banking he's referring to is so far removed from what I do, it's laughable. I guess that serves me right for misleading him in the first place. 'Thanks for the offer, Chris, but I'm heading back to Bath tomorrow.'

'Perfect. I could meet you there. Haven't been to Bath in a while. Might book myself in for some spa treatments while I'm visiting. I could book us both in, if you like? Let me know what day is good for you and—'

'Look, Chris, I work in a high-street bank as a cashier. I'm not in a position to do those kinds of deals.'

He closes his mouth and looks a little surprised. 'Okay. No problem. But I'd still love to meet up. A spa day could be fun? My treat.'

I sigh, realising I've been way off the mark. Chris wasn't behind the messages. Chris has come here tonight looking for a different sort of reunion. On paper, it would probably make sense for the two of us to get back together as a couple. He's rich, successful, handsome, good company, but our history is too complicated. I can't relax when I'm around him. The memories are too sharp. Too deep. It would feel . . . wrong. On the other hand, maybe I'm reading too much into it. He might simply be saying all this because he wants to get laid. Either way, I'm out.

'I just don't think it's a good idea,' I say with a regretful smile.

'Why not? I think it's a great idea,' he smiles back, undeterred.

I remember this about Chris – he never takes no for an answer. He's always pushing, pushing, pushing. It's how he got me to go out with him in the first place. But I'm not a pushover anymore. I'm a grown woman who knows what she wants. I'm just going to have to be firm.

'Sorry, Chris, but no.' This time, I skewer him with an unwavering gaze.

His jaw tenses. 'Fine.' He stands and walks away without saying goodbye.

I'm relieved he's gone, but the encounter leaves me rattled. The abruptness of his departure feels somehow violent. Chris Tamber isn't someone you want to piss off.

Rather than this feeling like closure, I worry that I've made him angry. That he won't let this go. Our past relationship wasn't exactly a healthy one. But then again, it wasn't necessarily him who called all the shots. Maybe I should go after him, check everything's okay. Make sure that we can leave here on friendly terms. But I'll let him cool down first. I've bruised his ego. I'll wait until it's less tender.

I sit and sip my drink for a few moments, pushing Chris Tamber from my thoughts and refocusing on Nathan Blake. I refuse to sit here and stew, letting Chris's temper ruin my evening. No. Like I promised myself, I'm going to shoot my shot with Nathan. If I don't at least try, I'll regret it.

'Everything okay?' Jas bounds over like an overexcited puppy and plonks herself down in the chair Chris just vacated. 'I saw you and Chris looking cosy. Where's he gone? To get you a drink? To call his helicopter so he can whisk you away to Paris for the night?'

'No thank you.'

'Ooh, you turned him down?' Jas quirks an eyebrow.

'Who turned who down?' Harriet sits down, scooching her chair closer.

'Chloe turned Chris down.'

'It's all water under the bridge,' I say, trying to downplay it. The last thing I need is for this piece of gossip to work its way round the venue. That would piss Chris off even more.

'What did he say?' Harriet asks.

'Nothing. He just asked if I wanted to meet up in Bath.'

'And you said no?'

I nod. No one knows what happened back then, and I want to keep it that way. I need to change the subject. 'What about you, Harriet?' I ask. 'See anyone here you fancy?'

She screws up her nose. 'Nope.'

'Harriet's still hung up on her mystery man,' Jas says. 'Come on, Harrie, now that we're here, all friends together, you can tell us who he is, or at least give us a clue.'

Harriet draws an invisible zip across her lips with her thumb and forefinger.

'Spoilsport,' Jas replies, sticking out her lower lip. She turns to me. 'So, is Operation Nathan still on?'

I tilt my head from side to side, unsure how to reply.

'That'll be a yes then,' she cries with glee, clapping her hands. 'First, we need to get him away from the coven. That is, if Abigail's perfume doesn't asphyxiate him first.'

Harriet snorts. 'How about if I tell Abi that Georgia needs help with the raffle? Abi thinks the sun shines out of Georgia's arse, so she'll love that.'

'Yes,' Jas agrees, her eyes lighting up. 'And while you're doing that, I'll tell Georgia that Abi and the others want to help out.'

'You two are so devious,' I say admiringly.

Harriet buffs her nails on her chest.

'Told you,' Jas says, 'we're your wing wonam . . . woman. *Women.*'

'You're so drunk!' Harriet says, laughing.

'It's a party!' she cries, before turning back to me. 'Right, give us two minutes to clear out the coven, and then you can make your move.'

I'm too tipsy and nervous to object. All I can do is watch as the two of them head off, giggling like teenagers. This whole scheme feels like something we might have done back at school. But how have I found myself back in such a – let's face it – childish situation all these years later?

I stare across the packed dance floor to the bar beyond, where Nathan is still chatting away to Abigail and the rest of them. Self-doubt starts to creep in. What if he really is into Abi and gets disappointed when she's called away? He might see me as an irritation. An interloper. Well, hopefully I'll be able to tell if that's the case, and then I'll back off. I just need a few minutes to talk to the man. See if there's any spark still there. If I don't try, I'll never know, and I refuse to leave here with any regrets.

I watch Jasmine pull Abigail aside and point over to the exit. They chat for a moment before I see Abi say something to Nathan, kiss his cheek and walk away with her friends in tow. Jasmine turns to me and gives an unsubtle thumbs-up across the room. I'm mortified, but it doesn't look as though Nathan is paying her any attention. His gaze is elsewhere.

I take a last slurp of Prosecco, wipe the corners of my mouth with my thumb, and weave my way around the tables towards him, my heart thumping louder with every step.

Chapter Twenty-Two

DEAN

I know I can't stay at the bar all night doing nothing but sinking pints. Despite the shots and the beers, my head feels remarkably clear, if slightly fuzzy round the edges. I told myself I wouldn't drink tonight. But the reality is that, without the alcohol, I'm not sure I'd have the courage to stay the course. And if I gave up now, I would definitely regret it. I spent too much time creating this opportunity; I won't let it go to waste.

My plan had been to stay hidden in the shadows, to not draw any attention to myself at all. But, having braved the bar, it's been surprisingly easy to chat to people. To lie about who I am. It helps that most of them haven't seen each other for years. That and the amount of alcohol being consumed. Of course, I'm under no illusions. This isn't going to be a walk in the park. I'm going to have to work hard to achieve the outcome I want. To get it cleanly and quickly.

I watch Tamber, fascinated and repulsed by the man as he moves from one group of friends to another, supremely confident in who he is and in how much these people adore and respect him. The sight of him enjoying himself after what he did . . . I have to take a breath to calm down. I can't dwell on all that now. I have to remain unemotional. It's the only way to ensure I don't make any mistakes. Anger will only cloud my judgement.

Despite Tamber's confidence, there is one chink in his armour that I spotted earlier – the blonde woman in the blue dress. He seems to be obsessed with her. I'd love nothing more than to intervene just to piss him off, but I need to hang back and remember why I'm here. I can't get sidetracked. The guy is an absolute dick though. She's clearly not interested, but he's not backing down, to her obvious discomfort.

A loose idea is beginning to form in my head. It might be a bit left field, but it could also be perfect. I blink and smile to myself as the makings of a plan start knotting together. I'm going to need to pick my moment carefully. This evening is going to be a waiting game. But I'll be patient. Because Chris Tamber absolutely deserves what's coming to him . . .

Chapter Twenty-Three

CHLOE

I edge my way around the dance floor, making sure to give Chris a wide berth as I head towards Nathan, who's now standing alone at the bar. I have absolutely no idea what I'm going to say, but hopefully I'll think of something by the time I reach him.

The closer I get, the more handsome he looks. Please don't let me make an idiot of myself. As I approach, I notice he's wiping away a tear from his dark eyes. Has he been crying?

'Hey, everything okay?' I ask.

'Huh?' He frowns, checks my name badge, and gives me a devastating smile. 'Chloe Flynn! How are you?'

'Good, thanks.' I smooth my dress over my hips. 'You?'

'Yeah, good. This is all very strange though. Being back. Catching up with everyone.'

'Very. We never really spoke at school though, did we?'

He pushes a strand of wavy hair out of his eyes, but it drops straight back down again. 'Not really, but I always knew who you were.'

'Same.' I smile, pleased that he remembers me. 'You haven't got much of an accent.'

'What? Oh, yeah. I guess I lived in the UK too long to pick one up.'

'So what's it like to be back in Bournemouth?' I ask.

'Nice, but also weird. It feels the same, but different, if that makes sense?'

I nod. 'Perfect sense. I moved to Bath years ago and haven't kept in touch with anyone, so it's really strange coming back. Although my mum still lives here, so I do come down to visit now and then.'

'How come you didn't keep in touch with everyone?' he asks, leaning close enough that I can smell his cologne – a warm spicy scent that cuts through all my senses.

I try to concentrate on what he's saying. 'Like I said, I moved away. Same as you.'

He smiles and nods.

'Hope you don't mind me saying,' I add, 'but you seemed upset a minute ago. Is everything okay?'

'What? Oh, yeah, I'm fine. It's just allergies. I think there's something in this hall that doesn't agree with me.'

I suppress a smile, remembering Jasmine's earlier comment about Abigail's perfume.

'Glad you find my pain amusing.' He smirks.

'Sorry, I wasn't smiling about that,' I reply. 'I was thinking of something else.'

'Hmm.' He gives me a suspicious look, but his eyes are twinkling and the corners of his mouth curl upwards. 'Anyway, even though I think you are laughing at me, I'll forgive you. Can I get you a drink?'

My heart skips like a pebble across water. 'Thanks. I came to get a Prosecco, but . . . do you fancy doing some shots?'

'A girl after my own heart,' he replies, turning to signal the barman.

Chatting to Nathan couldn't feel any more different than talking to Chris. Nathan is warm, open, and relaxed. There's no front to him. I get the feeling that what you see is what you get. Our conversation is natural, like we've known one another for ever.

And there's definitely more than a spark here. The air between us crackles. It feels like that split second just before the spark ignites and everything catches fire.

Nathan and I have been talking for a while, knocking back shots, laughing and teasing one another, when I spy Abigail Matthews heading our way with purpose in her step. My shoulders sag. I'd hoped to have more time alone with Nathan before she returned. Time for us to grow closer, to get to know one another better. I guess a busy reunion isn't the best place for a deep one-to-one conversation.

I take note of Abi's killer outfit – a fitted cream lace dress that skims her thighs. It has long sleeves that reach her knuckles and I noticed earlier that it's scooped at the back almost down to her bum. She's one of those annoyingly pretty women who has that effortless girl-next-door quality. It's a pity she ruins it with her bossy personality.

I don't want my conversation with Nathan to end. But I've already promised myself that I won't throw myself at this man or act with any kind of desperation. If Abigail wants to play it that way, then she can do just that. But I'm not fighting back or playing games. I'm ninety-nine per cent sure that Nathan likes me but if I've somehow got things wrong and he prefers Abigail, then there's nothing I can do. It doesn't stop me tensing up at her approach. Hoping with all my heart that he's been feeling the same chemistry between us.

'Hello, you lovely people,' Abigail says with a fake smile in her eyes. 'Chloe, it's so nice to see you here.' She steps in between us to air-kiss both my cheeks and I get treated to a waft of her overpowering rose-scented perfume. 'I see you've caught up with our elusive Nathan.' Abigail giggles as she bumps him along the bar a bit so that she's standing next to him and they're facing me, not a sliver of space between them, as though they're a couple.

Maybe they are, I think, my heart shrinking a little. Just because Nathan was flirting with me moments ago doesn't mean he's not seeing Abi.

Abigail gives me a thin-lipped smile, her eyes narrowing. 'So nice of you to keep Nathan company, Chloe. I've just been helping Georgia with the raffle. It's for a great cause – a local homeless shelter that gets people back on their feet.' She looks sideways at Nathan and smiles sadly as though she's genuinely touched, her eyes misting. I suddenly realise she's actually quite drunk.

'I'll make sure I get some tickets,' Nathan says.

'That's great. Thank you.' She places a hand proprietorially on his arm.

'Oh, of course,' I add. 'Me too.'

'You absolutely must,' Abigail continues. 'We've got some great prizes too – adventure days, dinner for two, an iPad . . .' Her tone changes. 'Chloe, could I just have a quick word?'

I frown, puzzled.

She beckons me away from Nathan and I give him an apologetic shrug before following her over to a quiet spot at the side of the bar.

'Everything okay, Abi?' I ask.

'Kind of,' she replies vaguely. 'But also, kind of *not*.'

'How do you mean?' I ask, sensing possible drama ahead.

'Look,' she says, trying to arrange her face into a serious expression. 'I know you and me . . . we have some history . . .'

That's putting it mildly, I think to myself.

She has the grace to flush before carrying on, '. . . *but*, I'm asking you, as a friend, for old times' sake, to give me and Nathan some space this evening.' Abigail says the words carefully, trying not to slur, but failing.

'Some space?' I echo stupidly.

She goes on in earnest, 'I think there's a real chance that me and Nathan – Nathan and I – might get together tonight. We've been chatting online and there's definite sexual chemistry between us. A real kind of tension. I think he could be . . . *the one*.' Her blue eyes are bright, excited. And then they darken. 'But you're not helping, Chloe.' She pokes me in the chest and I take a step back. 'Muscling in every time I get called away. If I'm honest, it actually looks quite desperate.' She tilts her head in faux sympathy.

'Muscling in?' I raise an eyebrow. 'I just came to the bar for a drink, and the two of us got chatting. I'd hardly call that "muscling in". And calling me "desperate" is pretty rich—'

'Oh, well, sorry.' She cuts me off. 'It just looked a bit like . . . So, there's nothing . . . I mean, you're not trying to . . .' Her hands are flailing all over the place as she tries to articulate what she means.

'He's a nice guy,' I reply, 'and we're having a fun conversation, a bit of cheeky banter. Nothing wrong with that, is there?' I'm not about to tell Abigail Matthews how I really feel about Nathan. Not in light of our history. She's always treated everything as a competition that she has to win at all costs. Looks like that hasn't changed with time. And alcohol has only intensified her need to beat me. 'Hey, Abigail . . .' I begin as something occurs to me.

'What?' she frowns.

'Was it you who sent me those emails?'

'Emails? No. Georgia did most of the reunion organising,' she replies. 'I just helped.'

'I'm not talking about the reunion invitation,' I say, watching her carefully. 'I mean the anonymous emails that someone sent me afterwards.'

'I have no idea what you're on about, Chloe. What emails? What's that got to do with Nathan? Have you been messaging him?' Her eyes narrow.

'No. Never mind.' I take a breath. If it *was* Abigail who sent them, she's doing a good job of covering it up.

'I saw you with Chris earlier,' she says slyly. 'You look good together, you two. I'm pretty sure he's still in love with you.'

I don't dignify that with an answer.

'Anyway,' she continues, 'you'll give me and Nath some space, right? Seeing as you're not interested in him.'

I love how she's putting words in my mouth. I never said I wasn't interested in him. In the past, I wouldn't have been so laid back. My claws would have already been out. But I won't make a fool of myself by arguing with a drunk Abigail over a boy. If Nathan and Abi really do have a thing going, then I'm not going to push myself on him. I grit my teeth. Abi has a bloody cheek after what she did to me back at school. Never mind that she probably did me a favour in the long run, I still don't trust her as far as I could throw her.

'Sure. Go for it,' I reply, patting her shoulder, before turning and walking away.

I like the thought that she was probably expecting me to put up a fight. That I've wrong-footed her. As I head back to the table, I don't so much as glance back in Nathan's direction. If he likes me, he'll come to find me. If he doesn't, I'll be gutted for a while, and then I'll get over it, like I always do. But I'm still nursing the hope that he'll seek me out. That he'll want to explore our connection further rather than having a drunken hook-up with Abigail Matthews. I can't help picturing Nathan and I jetting off into the New Zealand sunset together. Even if it is just a childish fantasy.

'Chloe . . .'

Not again. I glance up to see that Chris is walking at my side. I'm starting to think I should just call it a night and go home. There's no closure to be had here with him, no fresh starts with Nathan. Only painful memories and awkward conversations.

Chapter Twenty-Four

Chris drums the table repeatedly with his fingertips. It's driving Chloe mad, but she doesn't say anything. Her mind is on tomorrow's swimming race. She should be training right now rather than hanging out with her boyfriend, but he wouldn't take no for an answer so here they are. Seems like he's got something serious on his mind, but from the looks of him, it's not something that Chloe's going to want to hear.

It's a warm Saturday afternoon and they're sitting under a green-and-white striped parasol at a beach bar in Alum Chine, not far from both their homes. Only Chris's home is a multimillion-pound gated mansion, and her home is a tiny rented flat on a main road. He's never seemed to care about their difference in backgrounds. Chloe gets the impression he likes it. That he enjoys being her white knight, rescuing her from the drudge of poverty. He also likes the fact that she's pretty and has big boobs.

They've been an item since the start of Year 11. At first, she couldn't believe he liked someone like her. She thought it was some kind of prank that he and his friends were playing to humiliate her. But if it was a prank, it's lasted a long time. They've been going out for eight months now. Since they've been together, her school experience has totally switched around. From being a nobody who felt out of her depth to being a somebody who everyone wants to hang around with. It's a strange feeling. Like she's morphed into someone completely different. She wonders how she survived all those years beforehand.

'Chlo, are you listening?' Chris looks stressed. Is he cross with her?

Chloe tries to think about what she might have done, but nothing bad springs to mind. 'Are you annoyed with me about something?' she asks, fiddling with her new bellybutton piercing. She needs to remember to hide it from her mum when she gets home.

'I need to tell you something,' he says gruffly.

Chloe tenses. Is he dumping her? Surely not. She glares at him and he squirms in his seat. Anxiety chews at her insides.

'I did something stupid,' he says. 'But it didn't mean anything and I'm really sorry,' he adds quickly, his eyes pleading.

Chloe wants to cover her ears as she listens to him confess that he slept with Abigail Matthews last weekend. That he was drunk and she threw herself at him. How it had all happened so fast that he couldn't believe they'd done it. That he loves Chloe and would never do anything like that ever again.

Chloe wants to believe that, but she's not stupid.

She's gutted.

Chris made Chloe love him. And now he's cheated on her with one of the worst girls in the whole school. He's only admitting what he did because if Chris didn't own up, then Abigail would. Oh, yes, Abi and her friends will flaunt it in Chloe's face like a banner announcing how much better she is than Chloe. Abigail has always been annoyed that Chloe is even allowed in their school. How dare a lowly povvo like her be admitted to such a prestigious establishment. And how dare Chris Tamber fancy Chloe instead of Abigail stuck-up Matthews. It obviously goes against the natural order of things.

But Chloe has already seen how weak Chris is when it comes to girls. His eyes are constantly straying. Makes sense that his dick will follow, given the slightest hint of encouragement.

She's betting that Abigail only slept with him because the end-of-school prom is coming up and she doesn't have a decent date. Abigail's probably hoping that Chloe will find out about Chris's infidelity and ditch him so that she can then swoop in as his replacement date.

Chris has been on at Chloe to sleep with him for ages, but she wanted to save herself for prom night. Wanted it to be special. He and Abigail have ruined that now. She gulps down the anger and tears threatening to erupt. Her fingers are tingling with the need to let it all out.

'Can you say something?' Chris asks.

Chloe should yell at him. Should tell him to get lost. But if she did that, she'd be playing right into Abigail Matthews' hands, and she can't do that. Abigail is a troublemaker. Chloe's not going to let her ruin their relationship.

'Chloe,' Chris pleads. 'I really am sorry. What can I do to make it up to you?'

She bites her lip, refusing to cry and scream. At least he regrets it. At least he's looking for forgiveness. Chloe realises, with a jolt of understanding, that it's she who holds all the cards now. And she knows just what she's going to do with them.

Chapter Twenty-Five

CHLOE

With Chris at my side for what seems like the hundredth time, I'm scratching around for an excuse to escape. I don't want to be rude but as he isn't taking the hint, I'm just going to have to be blunt. 'Sorry, I'm just on my way to speak to Harriet and Jas.' I glance around the hall, trying to locate at least one of them.

'You can speak to them later, can't you?' Chris shakes his head, annoyed.

Despite my irritation, I stop and turn, waiting for him to say whatever it is he has to say. At least he seems to have calmed down after storming off earlier.

He stares at me. 'I saw you talking to that bloke at the bar.'

'You mean Nathan Blake?'

'Oh, right, is that who it was? I thought Blake left in Year 10.'

'He did. But he's come back for the reunion.'

'Always thought he was a bit of a weirdo,' Chris says. 'Anyway, I'm not here to talk about him. I'm sorry I walked off before but, well, the truth is, the only reason I wanted to come to this stupid evening was to see you.' He stands in front of me, looking more forlorn than I've ever seen him. This isn't like Chris. He's always been supremely confident, arrogant, rude even. He doesn't do sad or humble. Unless he's changed over the past fifteen years. Which I highly doubt, but I suppose is possible.

I pause, unsure of what to say. I'm not remotely interested in rekindling anything with this man. Aside from the fact he cheated on me years ago – which I forgave at the time – I can't ignore everything that happened afterwards.

'Like I said earlier, Chris, it's not a good idea.'

'But—'

I put a hand on his arm. 'Sorry, I really have to find my friends.' I walk off, feeling bad for him, but the alcohol in my bloodstream is taking the edge off my emotions, making everything feel fuzzy and not quite real.

'There you are!' Jasmine cries, as she and Harriet link arms with me, one on either side.

'Where've you been?' Harriet asks. 'We saw you getting cosy with Nathan earlier.'

'Why is Abi back there talking to him again?' Jas demands. 'What happened?'

'Is there some place quiet we can go for a minute?' I ask. 'I can't get rid of Chris and I need to sober up.'

'I know where,' Harriet says. 'But we'll need our coats.'

We swing past the table, where I grab my jacket, and then we make a mad dash towards the fire exit. Cold air hits me like a slap in the face, making me gasp. 'It's freezing out here!' I cry, my teeth already chattering. I'm grateful it's not raining too hard anymore. Just a few icy splats.

'Where are we going, Harrie?' Jasmine asks. 'We can't stay out here. It's too flipping cold and we'll get wet.'

'There!' Harriet points to the white gazebo lit up in the centre of the main lawn, fairy lights twinkling and swaying. 'Thought we could have a quick ciggie in the gazebo for old times' sake.' It was always a favourite spot to hang out, back in the day, usually commandeered by the older kids. It finally became our domain in Year 11. But its appeal isn't so great on a cold, dark November night.

'Okay,' Jas relents. 'Just a quick one though.'

I pull my jacket closer around my shivering body as we clomp our way along the path and up the steps of the octagonal wooden structure. Harriet takes a pack of Marlboro from her coat pocket and offers them up. Jas slides one out and crouches against the wind to light it with Harriet's Zippo. I never used to smoke because of my fitness, but I take one now, too drunk to refuse. I can't manage to light it though, and eventually give up, relieved as I didn't really want it in the first place.

'So, what happened with Nathan?' Harriet asks, taking a deep drag of her cigarette. 'After our brilliant plan.'

I tell them about how he and I were getting on so well before Abigail's drunken demand that I give her and Nathan some space.

'*What?*' Jas wrinkles her nose, exhaling a long stream of smoke. 'She warned you off, and you agreed to that?'

'Yep,' I reply morosely, wondering why I did agree. 'It seemed like a good idea at the time. I didn't want to deal with her throwing a hissy fit. Can you imagine if I'd told her to piss off? She'd have gone mad and then Nathan would have seen us arguing over him. It would have been horrible.'

'The nerve of the woman,' Harriet says, sucking on her cigarette until the tip glows bright red.

'You still should've refused,' Jasmine says. 'You can't let her get away with stuff like that! She's so spoilt, she thinks she can swan around ordering everyone to fall in line.'

'And then Chris accosted me,' I add.

'It's your fault for being so beautiful,' Harriet says, tapping me on the cheekbone.

'Ahh, you're sweet, Harrie,' I reply. 'But I think it's more a case of Chris wanting what he can't have.'

Once Jas and Harriet have ground out their cigarettes, they huddle closer and we have a group hug – partly emotional and partly to try to warm up – followed by a few selfies under the fairy lights. Pretty soon, we all agree that it's far too cold for any sane person to be out here without thermal underwear, so we hurry back into the hall, where the party feels as though it's ramped up a gear since we left. The music sounds louder, everyone's drunker, and there are now several couples snogging on the dance floor.

My eyes are drawn to the bar, where Abigail is still talking to Nathan. At least they're not standing that close to one another. Not yet anyway. He catches my eye, and my heart jumps into my throat. I really have got it bad.

'Just going to the loo,' I tell my friends, wondering if he might follow me out there.

'I'll get us another bottle while you're there,' Jas says before weaving unsteadily towards the bar.

I make a resolution not to have any more to drink. I don't want to do or say anything I might regret tonight. For more reasons than one.

As I reach the door to the toilets, Chris is walking out. He stops when he sees me and smiles lazily. I swear under my breath, cursing my bad timing. Anyone else but him would have given up by now.

'Chlo,' he says softly, his eyes slightly unfocused. 'It's fate. We keep running into each other tonight.'

'It's a small venue,' I reply, knowing full well that the only reason we keep running into one another is that he's following me round like a bad smell. I need to get past him, but he's blocking the entrance.

'Look, Chlo, I'm sorry about what happened with Abigail back at school. I was stupid and now you're punishing me. I get it.' He loosens his bow tie. 'It was a long time ago, can't we let it be water under the bridge? We're both here. I'm single, you're single . . . what do I need to do so we can skip to the part where you forgive me?'

'There's nothing you need to do,' I reply, trying not to snap. 'We're over now. We ended years ago. And that's that, okay?' I turn to head back into the hall. If he won't let me into the loos then I'll come back later.

'You're just being stubborn to pay me back for Abigail.' Chris follows me. 'It was a mistake. I already admitted that. You said you forgave me. She means absolutely nothing to me. Less than nothing.'

'I don't care about Abigail!' I cry, turning around to face him. 'I just want you to leave me alone.' My heart is racing and tears prick behind my eyes. Why won't he get the message?

'Maybe this will remind you of what we had . . .'

To my horror, he leans forward, pins me against the wall and kisses me. Panic makes me freeze. After a second, my brain clears and I squirm, trying to get free, but there's nowhere for me to go. His body is pushing against mine, his tongue trying to force its way into my mouth. I can taste whisky. Smell his skin, his aftershave. Panic drums in my chest. I'm trapped.

Chapter Twenty-Six

CHLOE

I can't think. I can't breathe. All I can do is struggle wildly as Chris tries to force a kiss on me. Kisses that I used to crave like sugar. But now I know better. He's too strong to get away from. Pinned against the wall with no way to escape, panic paralyses me, until my brain whirrs back to life. Instead of fighting against him, I give in to his lips, softening against his hard body until he relaxes. And then I shove my whole self against him and slip aside, wiping my mouth disgustedly with the back of my hand.

He looks surprised for an instant and then sneers, straightening up. 'You're such a prick-tease, Chlo. Fine, I get the message, you're not interested. More fool you. I would've treated you like a queen.'

I find that very hard to believe, but I don't respond.

He smooths his shirt and runs a hand over his hair. 'You could've had everything you ever wanted, but you've blown it,' he says, before heading back into the hall.

Once he's gone, my knees go soft and I crouch with my back against the wall for support, gulping in air. Tears slide down my cheeks, and I inhale deeply to stop their flow. I want to run right out of here. Go back to Mum's. No, back home to Bath. But I remember the women in the foyer saying something about locking the main entrance at nine. I'll have to go back through the hall in order to leave via the other exit.

Sucking in a breath, I push myself up on to my feet. I shouldn't let this get to me. It's just Chris frigging Tamber being an entitled arsehole as per usual. Hopefully, he'll keep to his word and leave me alone now. My lips feel bruised and my mouth still tastes of his whisky. I lick the sleeve of my jacket to try to get rid of the sour taste and walk towards the double doors that lead into the hall, thinking that he and Abigail would be perfect for one another. They should have stayed together back then. Although maybe even she doesn't deserve that.

A rush of warm air hits me as I walk back into the hall. The night is gradually unravelling – balloons have burst, streamers have been pulled from the ceiling and are now being trampled underfoot, make-up has run, clothing is crumpled, empty glasses and plates litter the tables. Sudden hunger pangs grip my belly and I realise I haven't eaten anything at all this evening. I glance over to my right. The buffet has been decimated, but perhaps there's something left that I could salvage.

'Chloe, are you okay?'

I glance up to see Nathan at my side. I must look an absolute sight. My trip to the bathroom was waylaid so I didn't get a chance to fix my hair and make-up. 'Hi,' I croak. 'Just eyeing up the buffet to see if there's anything left that's edible.'

'Doesn't look like it,' he replies. 'You sure you're okay?' he repeats. 'I think it's my turn to ask *you* if you've been crying. Or maybe it's allergies?' he adds with a gentle smile.

'Oh. I'm . . .' I put my fingers to my face, feeling tears on my cheeks. I realise my mascara has probably run, too. 'Oh. This is embarrassing. I did get a bit upset a minute ago, but I'm fine now.'

'Was it Chris?' he asks, his expression darkening. 'I saw him come back in here just before you.'

'We did argue, but it's sorted now.'

'Did he hurt you?' Nathan's shoulders stiffen as he scans the room.

'No, no, I'm fine. Actually, I think I might just go back and freshen up. I must look an absolute state.'

'You look good,' he replies. 'Just a bit of . . .' He gently wipes beneath each of my eyes with his finger. 'There.'

'Thanks.' I smile weakly up at him, warmed by his attention. Happy that he took the time to check on me. 'I really do want to freshen up though. But I'll come straight back. Will you still be here?'

'Right where you left me,' he replies.

'I won't be long.' I head quickly to the toilets, throwing glances over my shoulder to check I'm not being followed by Chris. But I get the feeling that Nathan will be keeping an eye out for me. I wonder if anything happened between Nathan and Abigail this evening. She's going to be mightily pissed off if he rejected her. With relief, I open the door to one of the six empty cubicles and step inside. But as I turn to lock the door behind me, someone flings it open.

Abigail.

Her face is red, her eyes narrow hate-filled slits.

'What are you doing?' I demand. 'I'm in the loo, you can't just—'

'I asked you *one* thing,' she cries, her face taut, her eyes wild. 'One thing. And you agreed. You said you'd give us some space. Admit you said that. Just admit it!'

'Calm down, Abi. What's the matter?' This is all I need after my horrible encounter with Chris. I came in here to get away for a minute. To compose myself, not to have to explain my actions to a hysterical Abigail.

'You know what the matter is,' she spits. 'I'm trying to get to know Nathan, but whenever I turn my back for a second, there you are, all over him. You're doing it on purpose, aren't you? You should just admit it. You never got over me and Chris and now you're trying to ruin my life.'

'Don't be so dramatic. I'm not doing anything, Abi. Right now, I'm just trying to go for a wee, that's all.'

'Why did you even come here tonight?' she cries. 'You don't live round here anymore. You don't keep in touch with any of us. You should've just stayed away. But here you are in your cheap blue dress and tacky highlights, deliberately going after Nathan to spite me. You're pathetic!'

'It *was* you who sent those threatening emails, wasn't it?' I say, certainty and fury building in my chest. 'I should call the police. I bet they'd be able to trace the email address back to you.'

But she doesn't seem to be listening to what I'm saying. Instead, her gaze is travelling over my dress, my jacket, my bag – like she's looking for something – until she stops and stares at my left hand, in which I'm clutching my phone.

'You need to leave Nathan alone,' she says, her fists clenching.

'Abi, you're pissed out of your head. Can you hear yourself? You can't order me around, telling me who I can and can't talk to. This isn't *school*. Well, technically it is, but you know what I mean.'

'I am not pissed!' she cries drunkenly.

'Nathan's a grown man,' I continue. 'He can decide for himself who he wants to talk to. You're going to be horrified tomorrow when you remember all this. When you think about how you've behaved. That's if you even do remember.'

She lunges forward and grabs my hand. I'm confused for a second, until I realise she's trying to get hold of my phone.

'What do you think you're doing?' I yank my hand backwards.

'Give me that!' She makes another grab for it.

'Get off!' My phone slips from my hand and skitters along the floor. We simultaneously dive towards it, both trying to be the first to get there.

'I'm taking it!' she cries.

'No you're not!' I gasp, fumbling but missing as she kicks it away and it spins further from my reach. I feel slightly hysterical, like I don't know whether to laugh or cry.

'Hello! Is someone in there?' a woman's voice calls out, knocking at the bathroom door. 'Why's the door locked? I need the loo!'

'This block's out of order!' Abigail yells back, scooping up my phone triumphantly. 'Use the one down the hall!'

'Abigail, did you lock the main door to the toilets?' I ask, trying desperately to snatch my mobile back, but she's holding it high above her head, waving it around to stop me getting close. 'Why have you locked us in here?' I demand.

She ignores my questions and marches to the next cubicle, where, to my horror, she drops my iPhone down the loo with a plop. 'You should upgrade your mobile, Chloe,' she slurs. 'I don't think that model's waterproof.'

'What the hell did you do that for?' I cry, pushing past her and peering down the toilet bowl to see my ancient iPhone lying at the bottom. 'I can't believe you did that!' I turn around to yell at her some more, but she's moved from my line of sight. I slip off my jacket and wince as I reach my arm down into the cold water to retrieve my poor phone, which I'm guessing is ruined. I seem to remember something about putting a wet phone into a bag of rice, but maybe I've got that wrong. And, anyway, where am I going to get a bag of rice right now? I could kill Abigail. 'You're bloody well going to buy me a new phone!' I yell. 'You're not getting away with this.'

The only reason I've kept hold of this phone instead of upgrading is that it has old voicemail messages from Ben that I occasionally listen to when I'm feeling low. Messages from back when he loved me.

A door slams shut and I hear the sound of what is, I realise too late, a lock turning. I push myself up and rush to the main door, pulling on the handle, but she's locked me inside.

'Abigail! Unlock this door!'

'Sorry, Chloe. I've put the "Out of Order" sign on this block for now. I'll send someone to let you out later. Or maybe tomorrow, depends on what happens with Nathan. Byeee!'

Trembling with frustration and anger, I check my phone, just in case, pressing the home button, but it's no good, the screen is defiantly blank. I can't even call Harriet or Jas to rescue me. How am I going to get out of here?

Chapter Twenty-Seven

Chris straightens his dinner jacket and poses with Chloe beneath the silver and white balloon arch. Their leavers' prom is being held in the school hall tonight – it's better than any local hotel they could have booked, transformed by swathes of white silk billowing across the ceiling, giving the impression they're inside a vast, luxurious tent strung with fairy lights, white balloons and silver streamers.

Chris's heart swells as he glances at Chloe in her tight silver dress that shows off her body to perfection. Who would have guessed that dorky Fishy Flynn would have turned into this goddess standing next to him? He can't believe he nearly blew it by messing around with Abigail. Abi's hot, but she's not a patch on Chlo. He pats the hip flask in his pocket. Everyone's brought alcohol tonight. The parents and teachers all turn a blind eye, probably because none of them are saints either. Aside from wanting to loosen up, Chris is desperate for another nip of vodka to stop the nerves taking over at what he's about to do.

He wants to do it, but he can't afford to get caught. First, because it could jeopardise his place at sixth-form college. But mainly because his father doesn't tolerate what he calls 'shenanigans'. And Chris specialises in shenanigans. It's what makes him so popular – that and his good looks and family money. But his father is old-school strict and isn't above taking off his belt to try to keep Chris in line. Not that that ever works. All it does is make Chris hate his old man even more.

After their photo's been taken, Chloe squeezes Chris's muscled arm and tells him she's going to catch up with Harrie and Jas in the gazebo. He squeezes her arse in reply, and she nips his ear with her teeth, whispering that she'll see him in a while. She totters off in her heels, squealing as she greets her friends. Chris waves at one of his mates, Marcus, and beckons him over. Tells him he needs a favour. Marcus Lee is always good at doing what he's told. It's useful to have friends like that.

Once the two of them have spoken, Chris watches Marcus go up to Miss Fenchurch, the IT teacher, who's at the back of the hall sitting at a table behind the projector. Marcus gets her attention and points to the corridor, gesturing wildly. Miss Fenchurch's eyes go wide, and she gets up and follows him out of the hall.

Chris exhales and grins.

He sidles up to where Marcus and the teacher were standing moments ago, crouches down and switches the USB stick in the computer tower that sits beneath the table. He hopes it will work. No big deal if not. But it'll be so funny if he pulls this off. Something to talk about, anyway. For years, probably.

Chapter Twenty-Eight

CHLOE

I don't know whether to laugh or cry. Abigail has totally lost it. What does she think locking me in here is going to accomplish? I wash the toilet-bowl water off my hand and arm with the gross liquid soap from the machine, which looks like yellow snot. I'd kill for a nice hot shower right about now, with my favourite Sanctuary shower gel. Nathan must still be out there, waiting for me by the buffet. Unless he's given up. At the thought of food, my stomach growls.

I guess Abigail will head straight for Nathan now. She'll probably lie to him about where I am and what I'm like as a person. She must be horrifically drunk if she thinks this plan of hers is going to work. If she thinks I won't tell everyone what she's done. My shoulders sag. She'll simply deny it and then I'll be the one who looks deranged. I head back into the cubicle to examine my face in the mirror. Dark circles have appeared under my eyes, my mascara has clumped, and my hair has frizzed from the rain.

I think about Abigail's bitchy comments – she called my dress and hair 'cheap'. I glance down at my outfit. I really liked it, but now that I see it through her eyes, I guess it probably isn't what you'd call 'classy'. Maybe Mum was right. But it made me feel good when I tried it on, so surely that's what matters? Abigail always was a snobby princess. I hope Nathan tells her he's not interested. But why would he do that? She's rich and she's beautiful. Okay, she might be drunk, but so is everyone else here tonight, including me.

I open my bag, unzip my make-up case and start dabbing concealer beneath my eyes, repairing my face. Once I've made myself presentable again, I'll hammer on the door and yell for help until someone hears me. I'm sure someone will come along and let me out, won't they?

I'm just putting the finishing touches to my lips when a loud banging makes me jump.

'Chloe! Are you in there?'

It's a man's voice. I freeze. Please let it be anyone other than Chris.

'Chloe! It's Nathan!'

I exhale, blot my lips, and run to the door, my heart lifting. 'Nathan!'

'Chloe, is that you?'

'Yes, it's me.'

'I can't open the door!' The handle rattles. 'Did you lock it?'

'No. Abigail locked me in!' I call back. So much for me not telling anyone, but I'm so frazzled I can't think straight.

'She did *what*?' I like the fact that Nathan sounds so outraged. 'She told me you'd gone home.'

Of course she did.

'I didn't think you'd have gone without saying goodbye,' he continues, 'so I came to check.'

My heart warms at his concern. 'Thank you! Can you get it unlocked? I'm pretty sure Abigail will have got the key from Georgia, if you can find her . . .'

'Give me a minute,' he replies. 'Don't worry, I'll be back.'

I pace the narrow space alongside the cubicles while I wait for Nathan to return. I can't help my mind spooling forward to a perfect future. Of Nathan and I as a couple, explaining to friends and family how we met. Of how he rescued me from the loos after a drunken ex-classmate locked me in there. It will be a tale we'll tell our kids and grandkids. Okay, I know I'm getting carried away, but I really feel that there's something between us. Something more than I've ever felt for anyone.

Moments later, I hear the sound of voices and the jingle of metal. Finally, the door swings open and I see Georgia and Nathan standing in the corridor. She's smiling while he looks concerned.

'Nathan said Abi locked you in!' Georgia cries, unable to suppress a giggle. 'Oh, she's terrible! She asked to borrow the keys for a minute, but I didn't realise it was to lock you in here! What's she like? It feels like we've all regressed to teenagers tonight, doesn't it?'

'Thanks for letting me out.' I manage a grin, not wanting to make a big deal of this. Now that Georgia's involved, this juicy piece of gossip is going to spread through the venue like wildfire. I've already decided to play it down and act like it was a bit of fun. Even though what I'd really like to do is shove Abi's head down the toilet after my phone.

Once Georgia leaves, the smile drops from my face. 'Thanks so much for checking on me,' I say to Nathan. 'I thought I was going to be stuck in here all night.'

'Abigail doesn't like you very much, does she?' he says.

I shrug. 'It's probably her guilty conscience.'

Nathan frowns. 'Guilt over what?'

I shake my head. 'Never mind. Let's not talk about Abigail or I might start getting annoyed again.'

'I can't believe she locked you in!'

'She seemed to think I was getting in the way of you two hooking up,' I say. 'But if you're interested in Abi, then I would never—'

'That's why she did it?' Nathan asks. He shakes his head before fixing me with an intense gaze. 'I'm not interested in Abigail.'

Heat flashes through me. I blink. My mouth goes dry.

'Come on.' Nathan takes my hand, leading me back towards the hall.

'Do we have to go back in?' I ask, feeling dread at seeing either Chris or Abi.

'What about the pool?' he asks. 'It used to be your domain, didn't it? Swimming academy, weren't you, if I'm remembering right?'

'Yeah. But we'll need the code to get in.'

'We'll get it from Georgia,' he says. 'She'll know it, won't she?'

Nathan's right, and we sweet-talk the code from a reluctant Georgia, who eventually gives in, instructing me to *please* not let anyone else in there. Nathan and I manage to sidle out of the fire door unnoticed before hurrying hand in hand along the pathway to the swimming-pool complex. A storm is building – the air static with electricity, tree branches groaning in the wind. The sound of crashing waves carries from beyond the cliffs, and indigo storm clouds gather overhead, parting now and then to reveal glimpses of a bright moon.

At the pool entrance, I punch in the four-digit code. The door clicks and we push it open, walking into darkness, warmth and the overpowering smell of chlorine.

Memories come rushing back. Fear, longing, hope, triumph, despair. A terrifying mix of everything I used to feel on a daily basis back then. The memory of my failed dream catches in my throat like a physical thing, preventing me from breathing. I shouldn't have let him lead me here. It's too much.

Nathan locates the light switches, illuminating the Olympic-size pool, the viewing gallery, and the vaulted ceiling with its wooden rafters. The place I've tried to forget for the past fifteen years. Why did I come here so willingly? To face my past? To put it to rest?

'You okay?' Nathan asks, his voice echoing slightly in the vast space.

I nod, unable to speak. Fighting through the panic.

'Shall we sit?'

I nod again, and he leads me around the side of the pool, ignoring the benches, and instead dropping down on to the floor to sit cross-legged. I join him, sitting with my knees bent to the side. Both of us stare out over the still blue water, occasional ripples marring the surface.

'I've really enjoyed talking to you this evening, Chloe.'

'Me too,' I reply. 'I remember you from school, but you never really said a lot. You were always quite . . . brooding.'

He laughs at that. 'You mean moody, right?'

I smile. 'Enigmatic.'

'Nice. I'll take it.'

'So, what do you do in New Zealand?' Talking to him is helping to calm me. Taking my mind off where we are.

'I used to be in property,' he replies, 'but I'm between careers right now. Trying to work out what I want to do next. I might even move back to the UK.'

'Not married then?'

He grimaces. 'Divorced. Which is another reason I'm thinking about a change in my life. How about you?'

'Well, fellow divorcee here.' We bump fists. 'And I work in a bank.'

'Cool.'

'Not really. It's not my thing. Only trouble being, I don't know what my "thing" is.'

'Join the club,' he replies. 'I feel like we should have a drink to toast to our unknown futures or something. I'll run back and get us one in a minute.'

Silence pools around us. The air is still and warm after the hecticness of the party and the wildness of the storm outside.

'So, what's the deal with you and Chris Tamber?' he asks.

I sigh and shift my position, trying to get more comfortable. 'It's an old situation that needs to be over,' I reply. 'I don't know if you remember, but he was my boyfriend back at school.'

He nods.

'Anyway,' I continue. 'Back then, before prom, he cheated on me with Abigail.'

'Aah,' Nathan replies, with a smile of understanding. 'That explains why she and you are . . .'

'Why we don't exactly get on,' I finish his sentence for him.

'So . . .' He gives me an undecipherable look. 'Is that why talking to me this evening is important? So that you can prove something to her? Do you still have feelings for Chris?'

'*What?* No. No way. I'm not like that. I couldn't care less about what Abi does, or who she likes. She did me a favour back then.'

'Just be honest with me, Chloe. I like you, but I don't want to be messed about.'

'The truth is . . .' I say nervously. 'The truth is that I came here to the reunion tonight hoping to talk to you. I always liked you back at school, and thought it would be fun to see if anything could happen.' My cheeks are flaming as he takes my hand and brings it up to his mouth, kisses my knuckles.

I want to kiss him so badly, but I also want to make sure he knows that Chris means nothing to me anymore. That he knows this isn't a game to me. I look him in the eye and say, 'I'm not and never will be interested in Chris Tamber. He's a dickhead.'

Nathan laughs. 'On that we can agree.'

'He's been coming on to me all night,' I continue. 'He tried to force himself on me earlier. That's why I was so upset—'

'He did *what*?' The smile drops from his face.

'It was just a kiss, but it was horrible. Scary, actually.'

'He can't get away with that!' Nathan's eyes darken and he puts a hand to my cheek. 'Are you okay?'

It's nice to have someone feel upset on my behalf. To have them stick up for me. Ben used to be the one to have my back. I've missed that feeling of safety. Of comfort.

'I'm fine,' I reply, because no matter how nice it is that Nathan wants to rush off and defend my honour, to mend this for me, I can't let him put himself in harm's way.

'I'm glad you're fine,' Nathan says, his body tensing, 'but what he's done is out of order. He can't go around forcing himself on—'

'Honestly,' I cut him off, regretting having mentioned it at all. 'I'm sure Chris has got the message by now. He won't be giving me any more trouble.' But, knowing Chris, I'm not sure if that's ever going to be true.

'No, Chloe. The guy's an animal,' Nathan says, jumping up. 'I'm going to have a word with Tamber, make sure he knows the score. Just wait here. I won't be long.'

'Nathan, no. Please don't. I shouldn't have told you about it.' I get to my feet and touch his arm. 'Please, just leave it. It's not worth the trouble. He's not worth it.'

'No, *he's* not worth it. But *you* are.'

'I appreciate that, but the thing is,' I say, starting to panic, 'if you confront him about this, then everything will just get ten times worse. He'll get angry, you'll get hurt—'

'I can assure you I won't get—'

'*Please*,' I beg, having visions of the two of them in a fist fight. Of split lips and black eyes, of everyone watching and blaming me. I'm praying he'll listen to me. But something in his manner tells me he's not going to let this go.

Chapter Twenty-Nine

CHLOE

Nathan's shoulders are squared, his eyes narrowed, his gaze still fixed beyond the doors.

'If you like me at all, Nathan, then please don't do this.' I stand in front of him and stare directly into his eyes, trying to get him to focus on me so he can see just how serious I am.

He finally shifts his attention back to me, and he must see something in my expression that convinces him not to go chasing after Chris, because his features start to soften. 'Okay,' he relents, his shoulders dropping. 'Okay. For you. I won't say anything to the prick. At least not here, tonight.'

'Thank you,' I reply, letting out a breath. 'Anyway, I think I'd better find Harriet or Jasmine, let them know I'm okay. My phone's trashed so I can't message them.'

'What happened to your phone?' he asks, his forehead creasing.

'Didn't I tell you?' I grit my teeth at the memory of Abi's unhinged behaviour. 'Well, not content with locking me in the loos, Abigail dropped my mobile down the toilet so that I wouldn't be able to call anyone for help.'

'Jeez!' Nathan's eyes widen. 'Looks like I had a lucky escape from the girl. We should hook her up with Chris – they're like this perfect devil couple.'

'That's what I was thinking earlier!' I can't help laughing.

Nathan's eyes crinkle. 'I'll come with you to find your friends.' He takes my hand in his. 'We can get a drink at the same time, bring it back to the pool, if you like?'

I nod and my stomach flips at the feeling of our hands entwined again. At the promise of what might happen when we return to the pool together. His hands are calloused, rough. He rubs his thumb across my palm. I'm going to tell Harriet and Jasmine not to wait for me tonight. I'll get a taxi back on my own. Or maybe even with Nathan, if things go well.

He opens the main door and we stand for a moment staring out at a sheet of rain. A flash of lightning whips across the sky.

'Do you still want to go?' Nathan asks, having to raise his voice above an ongoing boom of thunder that rattles my teeth. 'Or shall we wait for it to ease up?'

'I don't want to go out in that, but I should find them, really. They might be worrying where I am.'

'Okay, we'll make a run for it.' He pulls the door closed behind us and we dash back towards the main building hand in hand, laughing as we run.

We've only made it a couple of hundred yards or so along the path when we barrel headlong into a hunched figure.

I squeal, still giddy with laughter.

'Sorry, mate,' Nathan cries.

My heart sinks as the man looks up with a deep scowl on his face. *Chris.*

'Well, this explains a lot,' he sneers, glancing from me to Nathan and back again as the rain pelts down. 'You and Nathan

Blake,' he says. 'I thought I saw him sniffing around you earlier. What are you doing with this loser, Chlo? Trading down?'

Nathan steps in front of me, but I step forward too, scared of what might actually be happening here. Remembering a few moments ago when Nathan wanted to confront Chris. Looks like he got his wish, but I hope he remembers his promise not to do anything about it.

I pull at Nathan's dripping sleeve. 'Come on, let's go. We're getting drenched out here.' The rain has already soaked through my jacket and through my dress to my skin. Night briefly turns as bright as day under another streak of lightning. A following roll of thunder vibrates the air.

'You go back into the hall, Chloe,' Nathan says, his voice raised above the weather. 'This won't take long. I'll find you in a bit.'

'I'm not going anywhere while you two are behaving like idiots,' I snap, hugging myself against the cold sting of the storm.

'Speak for yourself and Blake,' Chris replies, wiping the rain from his face ineffectively.

'Chloe, please.' Nathan's voice is gruff, harsh. His eyes are narrowed and his stance is tense. He's taking this way too seriously. So seriously that it's starting to freak me out.

'Nathan, you promised you'd leave it. This is—'

'Told you he was a loser, Chlo,' Chris interrupts. 'He's all bent out of shape, and he barely knows either of us.' Chris shifts his gaze to Nathan and starts talking to him as though he's a young child. 'Hey, mate, you need to calm down. You're overreacting. Think you might have some anger issues.' Chris glowers at Nathan, but a confused expression has now come over his face. I want to ask him why he's looking at Nathan like that.

'I've been waiting a long time for this,' Nathan says. 'You might have been cocky at school, and you might be cocky now, but you won't be in a minute.' He spits out the words with real hatred.

I inhale sharply, suddenly noticing that Nathan has taken something out of his inside jacket pocket. 'What's that, Nathan?' I ask, an unnamed dread creeping up my spine.

He makes a small movement with his thumb, and a long, sharp blade appears.

'Jesus!' I cry. 'Nathan, what are you doing with that knife?'

'Whoa!' Chris takes a step back, his shocked gaze now trained on the weapon.

I can't take my eyes off it either. Nathan is wielding what looks like a hunting knife, long enough and sharp enough to do some serious damage. Maybe even kill someone. What the hell kind of person walks around with that sort of weapon on them?

'Why have you got a knife?' My heart batters my ribcage and my whole body is shivering with cold and shock. '*Nathan?*'

He doesn't reply. He doesn't even glance my way. He's wholly focused on Chris.

'Easy there, Nathan, mate.' Chris's face has gone bone white. He raises his hands and takes another step back.

Nathan takes a step forward. 'I'm not letting you get away with what you've done,' Nathan says, his voice barely audible over the rain. 'You've ruined too many lives. Including mine.'

'What the hell are you talking about?' Chris replies. But then he freezes and his eyes widen. 'YOU!' he suddenly cries out with shock. With . . . recognition. 'You're not Nathan Blake! You're Dean fucking Bradley!'

Chapter Thirty

It's a perfect summer evening – warm, with the scent of honeysuckle and freshly cut grass overlaid with a clean salt breeze from the sea. Swallows fly overhead, crying out to one another as they swoop and climb. The jewel-green lawn glistens beneath the gently sinking sun as a group of us clusters on the gazebo, having our photos taken by the official prom photographer.

'Okay, girls, that's it!' he encourages. 'Big smiles now. And . . . cheeeese!'

I wonder how I'll look in the photo. Happy I made it through? Relieved to be leaving? Excited about what's to come? Butterflies flap through my stomach and I exhale slowly.

I might look as though I'm enjoying myself – just another privileged graduating pupil of West Cliff School – but that's just it, I'm not the same as these girls. I'm a scholarship pupil who didn't quite live up to her potential. In the end, when it mattered, I let the pressure get to me. Not the pressure of the race. But the pressure of everything else. Of my life. Of how I'm supposed to live in such a hostile world. That pressure interfered with my focus. Made me doubt myself.

I lost my final race by two seconds, which means the sixth-form swimming scholarship I was hoping for at a top sports school in Somerset went to someone else. Like Mum says, it's not the end of the world, there are other opportunities, but it's made things harder.

Here we are, all laughing and joking, complimenting one another on our dresses, our hair, all that surface stuff. Pretending the popular girls haven't been absolute bitches for the past five years. That we're all suddenly such good friends, leaving on friendly terms. But the majority of my time here has been hellish. Trying to fit in. And for what?

Some of the younger years have been tasked with playing music or singing during this first part of the evening. Currently, a string quartet from the year below are performing outside the headmaster's study. They're really good. I don't recognise the piece of music, but it's emotive, melancholic. I feel a tear prick at the corner of my eye. Someone should probably have told them to play something more upbeat.

I blink back the wave of emotion. Right now, there's one solitary glimmer of joy on my horizon. A glimmer so bright that I can hardly dare to believe it might be real. I'm actually a bag of nerves at what's to come tonight. I press a hand to my chest to slow my breathing. Will it be everything I want it to be? I hope so. I've prayed for it enough times.

'The speeches are starting!' I glance across to see Mrs Patricks, the deputy head, beckon us inside, her fair curly hair loose around her shoulders instead of tied back in its usual ponytail. We clatter down the wooden steps and make our way across the lawn, back to the main hall.

The next few minutes are taken up with finding our places at the tables. A Year 9 student plays the grand piano, accompanied by a younger girl who's singing an Adele song. The tables have been laid with white linen tablecloths and silver cutlery. Even the chairs are covered in white silk slips. We're having a proper sit-down meal followed by a live band and then a DJ.

My table is on the opposite side of the hall, the closest to the corridor. But I don't mind. I like being at the back, able to see everyone rather than be seen. The pianist and singer have finished, and everyone claps and cheers. The performers smile at one another and make their exit while our headmaster, Mr Smythe, walks up on to the stage to the microphone stand, his tall, narrow frame and sandy hair so familiar as he's been here longer than all of us.

He clears his throat and nods to Miss Fenchurch, the projectionist, at the back of the room. 'Good evening, everybody.' His sonorous voice fills the room. 'It fills my heart with gladness to see so many of you wonderful young adults here this evening. Many of whom have been here since Year 7.'

A titter of laughter starts up around the room, but I'm not sure what he's said that's so funny.

'I feel privileged to have known each and every one of you . . .' Mr Smythe pauses, a slight frown marring his features.

More laughter, and the whisper and murmur of conversation spreads. Heads are all turning, looking, trying to locate something, or someone.

My skin goes cold as my gaze alights on the photograph emblazoned across the projector screen behind Mr Smythe:

It's a kiss between two pupils.

A girl's eyes closed in ecstasy as she kisses another pupil – another girl.

My eyes. My kiss. My love.

I remember that moment. It's imprinted on my heart. The happiness welling up inside my chest. Knowing that I had finally found my person. Knowing that she felt the same way about me.

But now I wonder in horror if it was all done simply to humiliate me. Her face is obscured in the image. It's only my *face that's on show for everyone to see. But it's clear we're both girls from the uniform we're wearing, our skirts and shoes and socks, her hair tied back in a ponytail.*

Why is it so funny to everyone?

My body has gone cold, but my face is burning. I swallow down acid and force myself to glance across the room to see her sitting at her table, grinning up at the screen too. Whispering to her friends, making them roar with laughter. Was the whole thing nothing more than a joke to her, a dare, a set-up? Did she never love me?

'All right, everyone, settle down,' Mr Smythe booms into the microphone, his frown deepening. He turns to look up at the screen and then turns back, glaring at Miss Fenchurch, indicating with a level hand and a sharp flick of his wrist that she should turn off the projector.

The screen suddenly goes blank and everybody boos and groans. There's more laughter. I want nothing more than to leave, but my feet won't obey me. I'm frozen to my seat.

I realise that everyone in the hall is either looking at the screen or staring at me. I shrink into my chair and stare resolutely at the table. But the image of the two of us is burnt into my retinas.

We'd agreed to meet up later this evening in the swimming block, but what would I find there if I went? More humiliation? More mockery? I'm devastated that this precious, intimate moment of my life has been put on display for everyone to laugh at.

But, worse than that, I'm heartbroken, grief-stricken, that the girl I love has betrayed me so cruelly.

Chapter Thirty-One

DEAN

Icy rain slashes my face, making me blink and gasp as I clutch the knife, holding it out in front of me so that it's clearly visible.

I take another step, pushing my hatred ahead of me so that it's quite obvious what I intend to do here tonight. That this isn't simply a threat. That I mean business.

My body is taut, the blood roaring in my ears. This is all unfolding more smoothly than I could have hoped for. Although I try not to think of how Chloe has been caught up in this. About how my feelings for her have taken me by surprise. I can't let her distract me. Not now that I have Tamber where I want him.

Despite the painful pounding of my heart and the sharpness in my lungs, I'm ready for this. I've already watched numerous videos online and read up about the different stabbing techniques – using a VPN on a burner phone, just in case. I practised holding this very knife in the kitchen of our family home, making sure my grip was firm. That I knew what I was doing so that I wouldn't fumble or drop it tonight. So that everything would be perfect.

But that was back when I was alone and calm inside a warm, dry house. Not out here shivering, riled up with alcohol and fury, with sweating palms and trembling fingers, facing the person who destroyed my life.

I jab the knife, driving him back towards the building behind us. To the swimming pool where it all happened. I memorised the code so that I could bring Tamber back here. To the place where my sister died. Where he, too, is about to get everything he deserves.

Chapter Thirty-Two

CHLOE

Chris's mouth hangs open in shock.

'Why are you calling him Dean?' I ask, gripped by fear and confusion. 'This is Nathan Blake.'

'No it's not,' Chris sneers. 'This lunatic is Dean Bradley. Or is it George Solomon?' Chris asks him, shaking his head. 'I can't keep up with all your alter egos.' He barks out a laugh. 'Am I the reason you came here tonight, Dean?'

I'm starting to realise that none of what's happening here is about me. These two have some kind of history together, but I'm woefully in the dark about what exactly that history is.

Chris turns back to me. 'You do realise I've taken out a non-mol order against this idiot.'

'A *what*?' I have no idea what Chris is talking about, but I don't like the sound of it.

'A non-molestation order. It's a civil restraining order. He barged into my office a while back pretending to be a client, issuing all kinds of threats. Word of advice, Chlo, don't employ this cowboy to build you anything – it'll fall down and you'll get a whole world of grief afterwards. This man is dangerous.'

Chris's words fill me with dread. Could this man really be dangerous? Have I fallen for an illusion? Or is Chris bad-mouthing him because he's angry with me?

Nathan shakes his head. 'You can't stop lying, Tamber, can you? You're a crook, a cheat, a thief and a murderer.'

'That's a bit dramatic, Dean,' Chris replies. He sounds unperturbed, but I notice his gaze keeps flicking down to the knife.

'Nathan?' I ask, my stomach grinding in fear. 'What's going on?' I realise that things have escalated so far out of control that I should probably run for help, but I worry what might happen if I leave the two of them alone. 'Why does Chris think you're someone else?'

'Because he is,' Chris replies. 'You can be so dim sometimes, Chlo. Does he look like Nathan?'

'*You* thought he was!' I snap. 'None of us has seen him for years.' I remember again just how much of a pompous dickhead Chris used to be. Still is.

'Well, as you can see, this man is dangerous, Chlo. You need to stay away from him.' Chris's gaze shifts back to Nathan, or Dean, or whoever he really is. 'You've dyed your hair, right? And shaved your beard? Can't believe I didn't recognise you, Bradley. Ten points for effort, but zero points for making the biggest mistake of your life. I'll make sure you go to prison for this.'

'Not if I kill you first,' Nathan snarls, jabbing the knife towards Chris.

I gasp at the threat. 'Why are you doing this, Dean?' I ask the man who moments ago I was daydreaming about spending the rest of my life with. His real name sounds strange on my tongue.

Chris answers for him. 'Because I wouldn't pay him for doing a shoddy job on my property. He's just a money-grubbing crook trying to get his version of revenge.'

'Turn around and walk slowly towards the pool building,' Dean orders, glaring at Chris.

Chris plants his feet and squares his shoulders until Dean jabs the knife at him.

'All right, I'm going.' Chris reluctantly turns and starts walking.

'Sorry, Chloe,' Dean adds, 'but I'm going to need you to come along too.'

I'm crushed. I know I should be scared that Dean is holding a weapon. That he wants to kill Chris, and possibly even kill me for being caught up in it, but I thought Nathan was the man of my dreams. I thought this was going to be the start of an incredible relationship. Now, I realise, I've stumbled into something that has nothing to do with me. This *Dean*, whoever he is, is here tonight because of some building project that went wrong. How seedy. How horrible. Was any of what he said earlier even true? Or was he lying to me? Using me to get to Chris? Disappointment drops into my chest like a heavy stone, making it hard to breathe.

I walk next to Dean without putting up any resistance. Maybe I can try to rescue the situation. Stop things escalating.

Chris comes to a halt in front of the pool building.

'Chloe, I need you to key in the code for me,' Dean says.

'Don't do it, Chlo,' Chris says. 'Run for help. Call the police.'

'If she runs off, I'll slit your throat right here,' Dean says to him.

'I'd like to see you try,' Chris replies, turning around and bringing his hands up to his chest and neck defensively.

Dean tenses as though he's about to lunge forward with the knife.

I can't let this happen. '*Don't!*' I cry. 'I'll open the door!' If I can just keep them talking a while longer, I might be able to think of a way to stop Dean. To get him to give me the knife. Maybe, on some level, he does actually like me. I can use that to stop this degenerating into something terrible. With wet, shaking fingers, I key in the code and push open the door.

Although it's only been a short while since Nathan and I stood in the doorway together staring out at the rain, it feels like a lifetime ago. In the space of a few minutes, 'Nathan' has become 'Dean', and all my dreams have shattered.

I stumble in through the doorway, shivering hard, my clothes dripping rainwater on to the floor.

Dean pushes Chris in after me and nudges him up to the edge of the pool.

'I'm sorry, Chloe,' Dean says. 'I know none of this has anything to do with you. But it's not what you think either, Chris.'

'Oh, it's exactly what I think,' Chris retorts, his dinner jacket shiny with rainwater, his hair slick, rivulets still streaming down his face. 'You're just a bitter little man. Jealous and insecure. A loser.'

'This was never my plan,' Dean says. 'I was going to do a claim through the county court for loss of earnings. Serve papers on you.'

'I'd like to see how far you get,' Chris sneers.

'But then I discovered something else,' Dean continues. 'Something far worse. And I realised that suing you would mean nothing.'

'Discovered something about me?' Chris is eyeing the knife, probably waiting for Dean's attention to slip. Waiting for a chance to wrestle the weapon from him or to make a break for it. 'Discovered what?'

I glance from one to the other and then down to the knife, terrified about how all this is going to end. I try to reason with Dean once more. 'Surely, whatever Chris has done, you're not going to hurt him? It's not too late to stop this. Just tell us whatever it is that's upset you, and we can try to fix it. I'm impartial. I can help.' Even as I say the words, I can see Dean isn't interested in a peaceful resolution. He's too keyed up to even listen. 'What are you planning to do, Dean?' I ask.

'Yes, Dean,' Chris drawls. 'What are you planning to do?'

Dean blinks and sniffs, wiping rainwater from his face.

'Are those . . .' Chris peers at him. '. . . brown contact lenses?'

Dean ignores the second question. He straightens and stares at Chris, his eyes dark with menace. 'Just shut up for a second, Tamber. You're going to stand there, and you're going to listen to me tell you exactly why you deserve to die.'

'Dean, no!' I cry. 'You're not killing anybody.'

'This should be good.' Chris crosses his arms, feigning nonchalance, but his jaw is clenching, and I can see the stress behind his eyes.

Dean's voice breaks, but he glares at Chris and manages to choke out the words, 'Laura Rudd was my sister and *you* are the reason she's dead.'

Chapter Thirty-Three

As I drop into the tepid water, Dad's words ring in my ears, pulse through my blood, harden my bones.

You're not my daughter . . . don't come back . . . how could you . . . shameful . . . what did I do to make you like this?

That night at the prom, after my face flashed up on to the screen, I somehow found enough courage to get to my feet. To flee from the hall. I ran home early and shut myself in my room without speaking to my parents. All I could do was cry and sleep and scribble in my new notebook. I poured out all my fears and desperation on to those pages. All the hurt and pain of thinking she loved me, only to discover it was a lie. The knowledge that my family will never accept this. Will never accept me. The loss of my sixth-form swimming scholarship to a faster swimmer from another school.

I know who took that photo because I saw them all laughing and congratulating Chris as soon as it became clear that this was a prank. But I also know that there's nothing I could ever do to make them understand that their idea of a prank was my idea of torture. They have no empathy. People like Chris Tamber always do what they want with no consequences. It's simply the way it is. If you complain or confront them, it just gets worse.

I push off from the side of the pool and I swim. Freestyle at first, following the black line slowly, powerfully, cleanly. And now I switch to breaststroke, then backstroke, but they're too sedate. Too gentle for the turmoil of emotions clawing at my chest and throat and brain. I swim a length of butterfly, pounding the water with my arms, feeling the violence of the stroke. But I can't keep it up so I turn at the wall and revert once more to freestyle, getting into a rhythm and speeding up. Until I'm racing for my life.

I barely left my room all weekend, couldn't speak to any of my family. I was too heartbroken. Too humiliated. Too scared. None of them knew what had happened, and I wasn't going to be the one to tell them. I prayed they would never find out.

Finally, I left the house earlier this afternoon to go for a run. To get away from the four walls of my room pressing in on me. But I knew that I was running to escape from myself.

When I got home, tired and breathless, Dad was standing on the front drive, two stuffed bin liners at his side, his arms folded across his chest. Mum was crying, pulling at his arm, telling him not to do this. Telling him to calm down. But he was *calm. It was Mum who was hysterical.*

'She's barely sixteen, Andy! Where's she supposed to go?'

'She should have thought of that before she shamed our family in front of everyone,' Dad said coldly, making my blood turn to ice. 'Respected teachers telling me all this filth about our own daughter.' He couldn't even look at me.

None of this stuff is supposed to matter these days. We're all supposed to have moved on. Live and let live. That's what everyone likes to think. But the reality hasn't quite caught up with the image of an enlightened society. It hasn't caught up with my dad, anyway.

So I stood there, shocked and disbelieving, as though I didn't understand what was happening, as though my father was speaking a foreign language. Yet a quiet part of my brain understood everything with crystal clarity.

It seems that, while I was out running, my parents decided to call the school to enquire what had happened during prom to upset me so deeply. They were worried about me. Thought I might have been assaulted, or had an accident of some kind. They spoke to the deputy head, who went ahead and explained everything that had occurred. Thinking she was doing the right thing. Thinking that my father would be sympathetic. That my parents would comfort me.

My dad loves me. He's a good man, a good father. But his goodness does not extend that far. His goodness does not extend to who I am.

Of all the ways I imagined coming out to my parents, this was not one of them. The choice was taken away from me by a well-meaning teacher who didn't have a clue about my safety.

The look on Dad's face as I stood on the driveway. The finality of his words: 'You are not our daughter.'

Perhaps if I'd been able to ease him into the knowledge over time, things might have been different. Or maybe not. To be honest, I'd planned on keeping it a secret for ever. On living a hidden life. A life that would keep me safe from this outcome. I know that many people have understanding families. Warm, open families who let their kids be who they are instead of forcing them to conform. But mine isn't one of those. Not as far as this is concerned.

Mum stared at me beseechingly as though I could fix it. Me. *What did she want me to do? Apologise for being bullied? Apologise for being me? I glanced up to see Dean peering out of our parents' bedroom window, his forehead creasing in confusion when I caught his eye. Why didn't he come down to stick up for me? Is he ashamed of me too? Is he mortified, embarrassed, disgusted?*

Unsure of where to go, I sat on the local beach for the rest of the afternoon with my bin bags next to me, sipping from a small bottle of cheap vodka that I'd asked a homeless woman to buy for me. I gave her the money, telling her she could get one for herself.

I sat there with the holidaymakers, the families, the couples, the normal people. I gazed at the sea, the sky, the sand, the seagulls, waiting for night to fall, trying to blot out everything else. And then I made my way here to the school swimming pool, the place that used to be my second home but has now become yet another sanctuary that's closed to me. Thankfully, the code won't change until next month, so I was able to stagger into the deserted changing room and rummage through my stuff until I found my new swimming costume. The one Mum and Dad treated me to before my big race. Before I let them down.

As I changed into my swimming gear and tipped the last drops of vodka on to my tongue, I coughed out a bitter laugh at the sight of the two huge bags of clothing I'd lugged here. They reminded me of that awful day when the rest of the swim team dumped my uniform in bleach. What I would have given then to have had a bag of dry clothes, let alone two of them.

Now that I'm in the water, I don't allow myself to stop and rest. I simply swim. My mouth is dry, my head pounding after an afternoon of sun and a bottle of alcohol that I have no tolerance for. But I'm in the water – the only place I belong.

I swim and I swim until my muscles ache and my breathing grows laboured. I push myself on. My foot cramps up and I start to cry, salt and chlorine, my throat constricting, my eyes stinging. I force myself to swim through it. I don't allow myself to think of any alternatives to this. It's too hard. Too exhausting. I can't do it anymore. Not like this. Not without her, without them, without anyone. The physical pain of exhaustion is nothing compared to all that rejection.

So I'll just keep swimming. Until. Finally. I stop. And I let myself go.

Chapter Thirty-Four

DEAN

'Laura Rudd?' Chris Tamber's face turns grey. His whole arrogant, defensive demeanour drops. He seems to shrink in front of me, the swimming pool behind him appearing to stretch on for miles. 'You're Laura's brother?' he asks, the air going out of him.

'Now do you understand?' I say, relieved that my sister's name is having this effect on him. That it's finally wiping the cocky smile from his lips.

'But your last name's Bradley,' Tamber counters, still not willing to accept what I'm telling him. Although I can tell he knows I'm speaking the truth. I can see it in the pallor of his skin and the fear in his eyes.

'Different fathers,' I reply. 'Laura was my half-sister.' I take a step forward. 'But she was still my sister, and I loved her. I still miss her every day. What you did was . . . cowardly. Cruel.' I sniff and wipe my nose with the side of my free hand. This evening has gone on long enough. I need to do this now. For Laura. For Mum. For me. I grip the knife tighter, as though it might spontaneously slip from my grasp.

I always regretted following my stepdad's instructions that afternoon to *stay upstairs while we talk to your sister*. Why was I so passive? Why didn't I come down and demand to know what was going on? Probably because I was tired and hung-over and I didn't have the energy to get involved. All I knew about any of it at the time was that she'd had a shit night at the prom and had holed up in her bedroom for a couple of days. The weather was good that weekend and I'd just finished my A-levels so I'd been out with my mates most of Saturday and Sunday, partying, relaxing, enjoying myself. I selfishly hadn't paid any of it too much attention.

Then they had some sort of bust-up out on the driveway and my stepdad told her to leave. I couldn't believe it. Laura was his baby, the apple of his eye. He was so proud of her accomplishments. What would make him so mad that he'd throw her out? A *boy*? Had she got herself pregnant? He was pretty strict and quite old-fashioned in that respect, so that would definitely have sent him over the edge. I should have got off my arse and gone down to stop it. To at least try to talk to them both. I was usually the one who got in trouble for stuff. I was the one who had stand-up rows with him for breaking my curfews or not treating him or Mum or the house with enough respect. It was a change to see Laura in trouble for once. Part of me had welcomed the change.

I loved my sister, but we were living in different worlds. She went to that posh school and was obsessed with her swimming, whereas I was a regular eighteen-year-old lad, enjoying life with my mates. If I'd known how unhappy she'd been . . . how miserable . . .

I assumed the whole thing would blow over, and she'd be back home by teatime with apologies. That there might be a week of sulking and awkwardness, but that things would eventually go back to normal. What I didn't expect – what none of us expected – was that there would be a terrible accident at the pool where Laura would drink too much and drown.

It was a terrible, surreal time that I've tried to block out over the years. Especially as my stepdad died so soon after from a massive heart attack. Everyone at the time said how sad it was that he had loved his daughter so much, he died from a broken heart. But now I think it was guilt and disappointment that killed him. Not love.

There were rumours afterwards about Laura being gay, and about her being humiliated during her prom night. But that's all they were – rumours. I'd thought it was just gossip, and didn't pay it too much attention. Not until last month when I found that notebook at the back of Mum's bedside drawer – my sister's diary, with some of Mum's thoughts written there too.

All of Laura's pain had been scrawled across those pages. The love she felt for a girl she'd met. A girl who had made her happy for a brief time and had then betrayed her along with Chris Tamber. Laura never mentioned any names in her diary except for Tamber's. When I saw his name written there on the page, I could barely believe it. *Chris Tamber?* The same person who had cheated me out of my livelihood and was trying to stop me claiming what was mine? Was this a joke? How could that man have had such a hand in ruining both our lives?

Sweat has started to bead beneath my shirt, on my upper lip and my forehead. After the freezing rain outside, it's too warm in here, airless, and my breathing is becoming shallow. I wipe the perspiration from my brow with my free hand and try to suck in a deeper breath.

Mum's diary entries were just as difficult to read as Laura's. Mum blamed my stepdad for Laura's death. She wrote that she was glad he'd died. But she also missed him. And that made her feel so guilty. Made her hate herself.

Reading my sister's and my mother's words was the most painful thing I've ever experienced. Almost worse than their deaths. I've been feeling quite unhinged ever since. Like I've been living in a bubble for all these years. Protected from the truth, when I should have been the one protecting *them*. Why didn't Mum confide in me afterwards? Probably because she wanted to spare me the pain. Or perhaps because it would have hurt her too much to put everything into words. Maybe she simply wanted to forget.

'Why did you choose to come here tonight, Dean?' Chloe asks, interrupting my thoughts. 'Wouldn't it have been easier to do this somewhere less public?' She's standing off to the side, midway between me and Chris, as though unsure where her loyalties lie. Perhaps they don't lie with either of us.

'Of course I wanted to do it quietly,' I reply, not taking my attention off Tamber for a second. 'But Tamber's a hard man to get close to – a gated house, a driver, security guards. And don't forget the civil restraining order he's taken out against me. He's got too many layers of protection around him. I get the feeling I'm not the only person he's pissed off over the years. So this reunion seemed like my only opportunity to get close.' I blink, wishing I could take out these lenses. 'It was easier to come here. To pretend to be Nathan Blake. No one's seen the guy since he was a teenager.'

'How did you know about the reunion?' Tamber asks.

'And about Nathan Blake?' Chloe adds.

I figure I may as well tell them. Now that I'm here, about to kill the man, telling him what I did won't make things any worse. 'I hacked your Facebook account.'

'You did *what*?' Tamber's face darkens.

'Yeah. It was actually really easy. I downloaded an app. Once I was in, I could access your account and see all your posts and messages. Your invitations . . .'

'How dare you!' Tamber splutters.

I continue, 'When I read Abigail's post about Nathan Blake, I decided that was my best bet. No one had seen the guy for years, he wasn't on Facebook, so I created a fake account as him and messaged Abi.'

Chloe is shaking her head, her wide blue eyes filled with disbelief and disappointment. But I can't let my feelings for her interfere with what I came here to do.

'You've lost the plot, mate,' Tamber mutters. 'I know you're upset about your sister, but—'

'Funny how you all accepted I was him,' I continue, cutting him off. 'I studied the old class photos you put up in the group. Dyed my hair, shaved my beard, wore coloured contact lenses and then posted my photo on Facebook. I swotted up on Laura's old classmates. Googled you all, read all your school memories on the Facebook group. Coming here felt like a no-brainer. By the time I arrived, I felt like I knew you all. Plus, there's a certain kind of symmetry to you dying in the same place as my sister, don't you think, Tamber? For you to know the same despair she must have felt. It balances the scales a bit.'

Tamber's throat bobs at my mention of him dying. I can't put this off any longer. He's showing no remorse. I need to end it. To end *him*. The only thing giving me pause is Chloe. I hadn't reckoned on us having such a strong connection. And now she's going to witness me murdering her ex-boyfriend. But I can't let her leave before I've done the deed or she'll call for help. If she does report me afterwards, then at least I'll have done what I came here to do.

I don't let myself think about the implications for Ellis. If I do, I know I'll walk out of here and go straight back home. But my sister deserves justice. I can't let this evil bully get away with what he did. I just can't.

I lunge forward, grabbing hold of Tamber's jacket with my left hand and thrusting the blade towards his jugular.

Chloe screams.

Tamber's arm comes up lightning fast to protect his neck and the knife slices through his sleeve instead, sinking into the flesh of his forearm. He cries out and tries to push me away with his free hand, but instead he flails backwards and topples into the pool with a splash.

I just about manage to keep my balance, stopping myself from falling in after him. The knife is somehow still in my hand, its blade streaked with bright red blood that turns my stomach. I want to let the weapon go. To let it drop to the floor and kick the thing away. But I daren't give it up.

'I'm sorry!' Tamber cries as he resurfaces, coughing and gurgling, the pool staining red as the wound on his arm leaks blood into the water. 'I'm sorry, all right? I shouldn't have done what I did.'

I stand at the pool's edge, panting, knowing I should go in after him to finish what I started, but I've lost the stomach for it. Chloe is kneeling at the edge, reaching out an arm to help haul Tamber out, but he doesn't come any closer. He's eyeing me warily, keeping his distance.

'I was a stupid kid,' he pants, treading water. 'I wish I could go back and undo what happened to Laura, but I can't. I really am so sorry, Dean. I mean it.' His voice breaks and he looks genuinely upset, but I can't tell if he's sorry for what he did or sorry for the mess he's in right now. Maybe he's just telling me what I want to hear.

'Not good enough,' I snap back. 'If you think a few tears and an apology is enough, then you're deluded. And it's obvious you haven't learnt your lesson since then. You're still swanning around Bournemouth, treating people like shit. Treating me like shit.'

'Don't you have a kid?' Tamber asks, gasping.

I clench my jaw at the mention of Ellis.

'What will it do to him if you get put away for murder?' Tamber glances down at his arm and winces at the ribbons of blood darkening the water around him. 'Chloe? Aren't you going to say anything?' he asks. 'Aren't you going to stick up for me?'

She opens her mouth to reply but I get there first.

'Leave Chloe out of it,' I retort.

'I didn't kill your sister,' Tamber calls up to me, his voice echoing around the pool. 'I know I didn't treat her well, but I didn't kill her. She did that herself. Maybe because . . . because of all kinds of reasons. Not just this one thing you're focusing on.'

Tamber's words are cutting through my rage. Slicing through to the heart of the matter. Because he's right. There were a lot of reasons Laura chose to end her life – Chris Tamber bullying her, rejection from the girl she loved, rejection from Dad, disappointment over her swimming scholarship . . . but the reason that guts me the most is that I was her big brother and I didn't stand up for her when she needed me. I let my little sister suffer alone. And that's all on me.

Chapter Thirty-Five

CHLOE

I can tell the fight has gone out of Dean. His body is trembling, and his face is pale. He's staring at the blood on the knife with something like shock in his eyes.

'Give it to me,' I say, holding out my hand, which is surprisingly steady.

'I can't,' he whispers. 'I have to do this . . . for Laura.'

'No. You don't.' I take a step towards him. 'You've done what you came here to do. You've confronted Chris and made him listen to you. He's apologised for his part in it. You heard him. He meant it.'

'But—'

'What about your son?' I add. 'Chris was right when he told you to think about him. What sort of life do you think he'll have without you? Knowing you're in prison for murder? That sort of thing can screw a child up.'

'I'll still be going to prison,' he replies flatly. 'Last I checked, attempted murder was a crime. So I may as well do the job properly and finish him off.'

'You don't mean that,' I say.

'Don't I?' His eyes dull.

I slip off my jacket and shoes, sit on the edge of the pool and lower myself into the water.

'What are you doing?' Dean cries, tensing up again. 'Get out of there, Chloe!'

I ignore him and swim over to Chris, who has moved further back to the shallower end so he's now able to stand. I try not to think about Laura dying in here. Drowning. The thought makes me light-headed. When I reach him, Chris is shivering with cold and shock, trying to keep his injured arm out of the water. His blood floats around us in whorls. My dress will be ruined.

'Chloe, come back!' Dean cries, pacing along the edge of the pool.

I really hope he doesn't decide to jump in.

'Not sure how long I can stand here,' Chris mutters as I approach, his face white and clammy-looking. 'Feel a bit rough. I need to lie down.'

'If I convince Dean to give up the knife, will you promise not to call the police?' I ask.

'No way,' Chris snaps, with a burst of energy. 'The man's a lunatic. He deserves to—'

'So you want to fight him? In this state? Risk getting yourself killed?'

'What I want is for you to get out of this pool and run for help,' Chris replies through gritted teeth. 'Call the police, an ambulance. Get that dickhead arrested.'

'And rake everything up again?' I spit. 'Is that what you really want, Chris? To give a statement to the authorities about what went down at our prom fifteen years ago? The papers will have a field day, what with you being who you are.'

'What are you two talking about?' Dean calls out agitatedly. He walks around the edge of the pool, trying to get closer, but we're standing almost in the centre. He'll have to get into the water with us if he wants to be part of our conversation. And I do not want that to happen.

'Chris,' I hiss at my idiot ex-boyfriend. 'I'm telling you it would be a bad idea to call the police. And if we don't sort this out, like *now*, Dean is going to swim over here with that knife of his and sort it out his way. So, I'm asking you, for old times' sake, to let this go.'

'And I'm telling you that you already owe me a hell of a lot,' he snaps back, grimacing with pain.

'I don't owe you anything.' I clench my fists and draw nearer to him until I'm close enough to whisper in his ear.

His face suffuses with colour. 'You little bitch,' he snarls.

'It's your choice,' I reply, my heart thumping, hardly believing I had the guts to say that.

'Fine,' he replies, scowling.

I give him a nod, and swim back to Dean, hoping to God that my long shot paid off, and that Chris will keep his word. Because if he doesn't, then we'll all be finished.

Chapter Thirty-Six

DEAN – 4 MONTHS LATER

It's finally stopped raining. The weak March sun makes a welcome appearance as I work the mini digger, scooping earth and dumping it on to the lawn, ready to wheelbarrow out to the skip on the driveway once I'm done. It's quite a fun job and I've promised Ellis that he can have a go when he gets home from school, before it gets dark. I'm excavating a pit for the foundations to the new extension that we're adding to the house.

That night at the reunion, after I'd confronted Chris and . . . well . . . after I'd attacked him, I'd been certain I was heading for prison. After all, I'd tried to kill the guy. Had sliced open his forearm. Surely it was a foregone conclusion that Ellis was about to grow up without his father, and that we'd lose Mum's house as well as the flat. I'd also been certain that I'd found the love of my life that night. And lost her again.

But none of those things happened.

Instead, everything turned around.

Somehow, Chloe persuaded me not to hurt Chris further. To let that night be an end to it. To let the past go. She asked me if it was what Laura would have truly wanted. She made me think of the impact it would have on Ellis if his father became a murderer. If she hadn't been with me, there's no doubt in my mind that either Tamber or myself would have been seriously injured that night, if not killed. Miraculously, Chloe also persuaded Tamber not to call the police. He had been quiet, morose even, when he climbed out of the pool, but he seemed genuine about not calling the authorities. 'She was your sister, I get it,' he'd said as he'd clutched his blood-soaked arm.

Even more unbelievably, Chloe got Tamber to drop the civil suit and to pay up what he owed me. Not just two-thirds of the payment, like I'd requested when I visited him in his office that time, but the whole damn lot. She was nothing short of spectacular. I can't even imagine what situation I would be in now if she hadn't been there with me at the reunion that night. I think she might just have saved my life.

That huge chunk of cash from Tamber has meant I can keep Mum's house and get back to working for myself again. I felt like Father Christmas last December when I visited my electrician, plumber, roofer, plasterer and all my ex-employees with an explanation and a cheque. I don't think they believed the cheques would actually cash. I'm still pinching myself that it happened. I was so relieved, not only for me, but for everyone else who had worked on the job. I knew how it felt to do an honest week's work and be reliant on a payment that doesn't come through. It's scary. And to be able to get the money to everyone just before the holidays was the cherry on top. I've gone from being a local pariah to being everyone's best friend.

I asked Chloe how she managed it, but all she would say is that Tamber did it for old times' sake. Because he still had a soft spot for her. I get the feeling there was more to it than that, but she didn't elaborate and, whatever the reason, I'm beyond grateful to have that whole terrible situation behind me. I feel as though I was overtaken by some kind of madness.

I turn off the digger and climb out, surveying my handiwork. Still a lot to do, but not bad for a first go at it. I make my way back into the house, gasping for a mug of strong tea and a couple of biscuits to dunk. The kitchen feels nice and warm after being out in the chilly spring wind. I wash my hands and stretch out the kinks in my neck.

The boiling kettle sounds like I feel – bubbling over with happiness. And not just because I've been able to get my finances back on track. After weeks of apologising and trying to prove my worth, of trying to show her that the real me is not that revenge-crazed man at the pool, Chloe eventually decided to give me a chance. To give *us* a chance.

I knew she'd felt the spark between us that night, but then everything got twisted and out of hand when we bumped into Tamber after leaving the pool together. As soon as I saw him there, I was unable to hold back my rage. I lost all reason when I thought about how he terrorised my sister until she couldn't bear it any longer. It still makes me sick with anger to think about how his cruelty helped drive Laura to suicide. But, like Chloe said, maybe our encounter will make Tamber think twice before he treats another human with such thoughtlessness. Personally, I'm not sure he'll ever change, but it's not my job to reform him. Confronting him was simply something I had to do.

Neither Chris nor I got exactly the outcome we initially desired. I had wanted to avenge both Laura and myself by hurting Tamber. And Tamber had wanted to withhold my payment and ruin my business. Ruin my life. I'm thankful that the most important outcome of that night, the one thing I got that Tamber didn't, was Chloe's love. And that was the best outcome of all. For me, for her, and hopefully for Ellis.

I've noticed that my son is finding it a little hard to adjust to her presence in our lives. I think he might be a bit jealous that my attention is also on someone else, which is understandable. Chloe has been amazing with him though. She's patient and sweet, so I'm sure he'll come around soon.

I never thought I'd find love again – or anything even approaching it. Whenever I'd pictured myself finding a new partner, it had been an abstract thing – a wife for me, a mother for Ellis, someone to share the chores with. What I didn't imagine was finding a soulmate. Someone I feel completely at ease with. Someone I can laugh with and who has seen me at my absolute worst, but still loves me anyway.

Chloe is gentle, kind, clever and fun. Like me, she's also been through a traumatic divorce, finding it hard to trust again. I'm hoping the two of us can break down walls together. Literally as well as figuratively, as she's going to help me renovate the house. In fact, she's going to be moving in with us just as soon as she's packed up her flat in Bath and found some tenants. I can't wait for us to begin our new life together. It's all been a bit of a whirlwind. The intensity of the reunion speeding up our relationship. Bonding us. She saw the darkest parts of me and yet she loved me anyway. She steered me away from a cliff, stopped me making the biggest mistake of my life, and then she sorted out Tamber and got my career back on track. She literally brought me back from the brink. The woman is an angel. My angel.

I grab a couple of custard creams and take my tea upstairs to survey my morning's work from above. Get a proper view of it. Crunching a biscuit, I push open the door to Laura's bedroom, which looks out over the back garden. I cross the room to the large window and stare down at the hole. Not bad. I've managed to get quite a bit done, but it'll take a few more days yet. I sip my tea and the steam mists up the window.

I turn away from the view of the garden and gaze around Laura's room. I still can't bring myself to sleep in here, preferring to crash on the sofa downstairs each night in front of the TV. That will have to change when Chloe moves in. I think I'll have to bite the bullet and redecorate Mum's room for the two of us.

Now that I've decided to properly move on with my life, I think it might be time to redecorate Laura's room too and make it beautiful again. Turn it into a cheerful guest room, or a smart office. Somewhere purposeful and happy. Somewhere free of secrets.

I think maybe if my stepdad, Andy, hadn't died so soon after Laura, my parents would eventually have redecorated her room. Turned it into an office or a craft room – Mum loved to sew. But with the death of Andy so soon after Laura, I think it was just too much for Mum. Too painful to think of packing up my sister's stuff too. So the room has just sat here, unchanged and unused. Mum made sure to keep it clean, but everything else remains as it was, trapped in time. Her bed by the window, the band posters on her walls – Snow Patrol, Foo Fighters, The Ting Tings . . . even though I knew she loved *High School Musical* best. All her swimming paraphernalia – the medals and trophies, goggles, training equipment.

My sister was always a quiet person, driven and focused. But there was this secretive melancholy about her that I never understood until the end, when I finally realised what she'd hidden from us.

The guilt I carry around with me is as wide as the sky and as heavy as lead. It will never leave me. I'm still so utterly shattered that she didn't think she could confide in me, her brother. That I wasn't there for her in a meaningful way. That her truth came out in the brutal way it did, without her knowledge or control. That my stepfather wasn't able to accept his daughter for who she was. Not until it was too late for him to say sorry and beg her forgiveness.

That's why I'm determined to be as open as possible with Ellis and any future children I may have. So that they know, whoever they are, they can be happy and confident. They can be free to be themselves, and I will love them.

Chapter Thirty-Seven

CHLOE

'Oh, hold on a minute, Ellis. Don't pour the flour in just yet; I'll find us a sieve.'

Ellis ignores me, dumping the flour into the bowl and staring at me as if challenging me to tell him off. Puffs of flour cloud around his face where he's been so vigorous, and he looks like a vengeful ghost.

'Oh, well, that's okay,' I say with a smile. 'We don't need to sieve it. It's just handy to get the lumps out, that's all.'

'When we make fairy cakes, me and Daddy do it like this.' He takes the wooden spoon and starts stirring the mixture crossly. 'We don't use a *sift*.'

'Great, we'll do it that way,' I reply, keeping my voice light. 'Everyone has their own way of doing things,' I continue. 'It's what makes us individual.'

He keeps stirring, acting as though he hasn't heard me. The two of us are spending the afternoon baking and icing fairy cakes together, but it's been a bit trickier than I anticipated. I'm normally great in the kitchen, but baking with a five-year-old requires a different set of skills.

When Dean and I first got together, I'd naively thought that his son and I would hit it off immediately. That I would quickly become the mother he'd never really had. But Ellis is still quite resistant to me. To the idea of me. I think, because it's been just him and his dad on their own for so long, that it's been a shock for him to have to share his father. I totally get that. When I was young, the couple of times Mum had brought a man home, I'd hated it. Had felt sick with fear that he would steal all Mum's affection and start bossing me around. Of course, now I'd love it if she had someone to share her life with. But I know Ellis and I will get there eventually. It's only been a few months since Dean introduced us. I'm determined to show him that I would never come between him and his father. That I want to make their lives better, not worse. That we could be a happy family.

But right now, he's not happy. Not at all.

Somehow, the two of us manage to produce a lovely batch of cakes without any tears or tantrums on either part, and we've boxed half of them up to take next door to Marilyn Parsons, who's ill in bed with a bad cold.

'Are you holding it tightly?' I ask.

Ellis nods, demonstrating how carefully he's carrying the Tupperware box by holding it out for my inspection, his blue eyes narrowed as though daring me to criticise.

'Lovely!' I reply.

This errand of mercy to visit Marilyn was Ellis's idea. He told his dad that we should make Mrs Parsons some cakes or biscuits to cheer her up because that's what Granny always used to do. Knowing how much I love to cook and bake, Dean suggested that Ellis and I could bake together as it would be a good opportunity for the two of us to bond. Dean, meanwhile, is visiting a few builders' merchants to get supplies, blissfully unaware of Ellis's mission to oust me from my spot at Dean's side. I haven't wanted to worry

Dean by telling him just how tricky things are with Ellis. I'm hoping that it won't be necessary. That I'll be able to win him round eventually. I might have to try bribery next.

Ellis and I leave the house and head next door, taking Marilyn's spare key with us so she doesn't have to get out of bed to let us in. She's a nice lady, if perhaps a little overbearing, treating Dean's home like it's her own. But she's an old family friend who Dean and Ellis have relied on quite heavily, so I guess she's almost part of the family. Part of a family that I'm going to be joining.

My heart swells as I think about my future. I managed to let my Bath apartment to a nice professional couple who were thrilled by the flat's high ceilings and wonderful views. I've quit my job at the bank and I'm going to live off my rental income until I decide what to do next.

So, I've returned to Bournemouth – a place I never thought I'd move back to – and have now moved in with Dean and Ellis. It sounds unbelievable, but the trauma of the reunion brought the two of us closer together. There's been a lot to talk about, not least the fact that Dean is actually blond-haired and blue-eyed! After the reunion, he cut his hair really short and he's now growing out the dark colour. And, apparently, he normally has a beard – which I'm not too sure about – but it's more like scruffy stubble at the moment, which is actually pretty hot.

Hair colouring aside, I'm happier now than I've ever been in my life. Dean got down on one knee and proposed to me earlier this month during a romantic evening walk on the beach. It's been fast but, like Dean said, *when you know, you know*. Of course I said yes, and we both ended up crying and laughing and getting our feet soaked by an errant wave. So we had to dash home to change before going out again to celebrate with our friends.

Jas, Ash and Harriet came to the bar that night, along with a raucous group of Dean's friends, who all seemed lovely – mostly married couples who are delighted for him and have been so welcoming to me. They all berated Dean for having been such a recluse over the past few years. For turning down their invitations to dinner and drinks and birthday parties. They made me promise to get him to be more sociable. It's nice to be thought of as popular and outgoing – I haven't had that feeling in so long. But now I'm blessed with this ready-made friendship circle. A warm group of people who want to welcome me into their fold. It's an incredible feeling. However, I've learnt from past mistakes not to rely purely on my partner for friends, so I'll make my own connections too. I have Jas and Harrie, and we've already met a few of their group. I'm going to throw myself into life here. Gone are the days of moping about and feeling sorry for myself.

Dean and I are getting married next year, after the house is finished. We've even discussed having more children so that Ellis can have siblings. My old life with my ex-husband feels like a pale imitation of happiness when I compare it to this new multicolour life with Dean. This is the real deal. Full-blown love with all the trimmings.

We're building an extension on the back of the house right now so everything is chaotic, a mess, but it's also exciting, creative. Mum has been keen to offer up her interior design insights, the latest one being a Mediterranean-themed balcony off the master bedroom, which is actually not a bad idea. Mum is thrilled with my move back home, although she'll never admit it. She also seems to like Dean and was very taken with Ellis. Of course, she's still ladling a tonne of unwanted relationship advice on me, but I employ my usual technique of listening while not really listening.

I open our neighbour's wooden front door and call up the stairs. 'Hi, Marilyn! It's only us! Ellis and Chloe!' I turn to Ellis. 'Why don't you run on up, and I'll make Mrs Parsons a cup of tea to go with those cakes.'

Ellis does as I suggest while I head into Marilyn's compact kitchen, feeling like a good person. Like someone who is neighbourly and full of community spirit. Someone who always does the right thing, rather than keeping herself to herself, unwilling to get involved. I make a pact with myself to become this type of person for real. Family oriented. A good neighbour. A loving wife. A doting mother. A loyal friend. It's easy to be a good person when you have time, money and the support of others around you. Others who want the best for you, rather than always putting you down.

I locate the tea things and start tidying the kitchen while I wait for the kettle to boil. It's clear that Marilyn keeps a clean and tidy house, but there are a few empty bowls and plates in the sink, some crumbs on the side, and the bin is full. I'll empty it on my way out. She must be feeling too poorly to keep on top of it all.

Marilyn has been in this house for decades, so she knows everything that happened with Dean's family. All the drama and heartache. Apparently, she's been really good to Dean and his mum over the years. A lifeline after Laura died, and then her dad.

When Dean and I started to get serious, he asked me if I'd known his sister back when I was at school, what with us being in the same year and both in the swimming academy, and especially as I was Chris's girlfriend at the time. Dean asked if I'd been aware of Chris's bullying. If I had done anything to try to put a stop to it. Not that Dean was accusing me of anything, but he just wanted my perspective.

I told Dean that what happened to Laura was the main reason I'd ended things with Chris. It was a horrible time. A time I'd tried to put out of my mind. I couldn't imagine what Dean must have gone through back then, and again, more recently, after he'd found the diary. Dean said that he wants to put the past behind him too. He said that we both deserved a fresh start after all the sadness and trauma. I agreed. And we've been true to our word. Looking to the future rather than the past.

The kettle boils and I make two mugs of tea, putting them on a tray with three Aynsley China plates. I add a glass of fresh water, in case Marilyn's thirsty, and make my way up the stairs to her bedroom, where I can hear Ellis chatting happily away to her. I hope that one day soon he'll talk like that with me. Confide all his hopes and fears, all his day-to-day worries and thoughts. I would love nothing more than that.

The only real dark spot in my life now is that those nasty emails have started up again. At first, I was convinced they were from Abigail. I thought she was the most likely suspect since she must be aware that 'Nathan' and I are now together. I wonder how much she knows about all that? Whether she knows that he wasn't Nathan after all. She must have been furious that he fell for me instead of her, and that could have given her a reason to start up with the messages again. So pathetic, but not worth responding to. I hoped she would simply get bored and give up.

But the latest couple of emails have been more personal. More explicit. More obvious. So I don't think it's Abigail after all. It's someone worse. Someone who has the power to take away my happiness. I pause outside Marilyn's bedroom door, trying to calm my breathing. What if they decide to escalate things, to take it further? What will I do then? I can't live with that kind of fear and uncertainty over my head. And I daren't go to the police, because I can't be sure that wouldn't kick-start the process of unearthing old secrets. Secrets that could be devastating for me if they ever came to light . . .

Chapter Thirty-Eight

Laura Rudd's funeral is being held at Parkstone Cemetery. Everyone is here – pupils, teachers, family. They've all come to mourn the loss of a talented young girl who died in a tragic accident. An accident that may not have been an accident at all.

Chloe realises that they've probably all colluded in this. The pupils, the teachers, even Laura's parents. No one has so much as hinted that it could have been anything else but an accident – a late-night swim alone, a cramp in her leg, her bloodstream full of alcohol. No whisper that Laura might have been driven to do something desperate.

No. It's far better for everyone to believe that it was, in fact, an accident.

Chloe sheds tears along with everyone else. Laura's death has been a terrible shock to the whole community. A tragedy. It was even on the local news – Rising Swimming Star Dies in Tragic Accident *– with an accompanying photo of Laura holding a trophy. A trophy that Chloe had coveted at the time. But there was no denying that Laura's talent had wildly surpassed Chloe's. Chloe had never had the opportunity to shine at West Cliff School. Not while Laura was stealing the show.*

As they stand at the graveside, Chloe's heart has begun to beat a little too fast, a little too hard. She's nervous that everything is going to come out. It's common knowledge at school that it was Chris who took the photo and switched the USB sticks, because he was bragging about it on the night, and everyone said it was hilarious. A few of the kids thought it was mean, but only because they were losers too, and had likely been victims of similar pranks. But people like Chris can get away with stuff like that because of who they are. Because of how much money his family donates to the school. If it had been anyone else, Chloe is certain that nothing would have been brushed under the carpet. That there would have been investigations and pupils being hauled up in front of the headmaster. But there was none of that. There was just this resounding silence. So, yes, with his rich-kid immunity, Chris had initially enjoyed being congratulated as the genius behind such an awesome stunt.

Even though he wasn't the one behind it at all.

Because the whole projector-screen plan had been Chloe's idea.

She'd been jealous of Laura's athletic ability. From the moment they joined the swimming academy in Year 7, it was clear Laura Rudd was better than the rest of them. More gifted, more focused, harder working.

As Chloe stands here mourning the loss of her rival, she's ashamed to acknowledge that she'd made Laura's life a misery. Chloe was never the most popular student in the year, but she always had a knack for making up creative ways to intimidate and humiliate anyone who trod on her toes – like stealing their clothes and dumping them in a bucket of bleach. That had actually been quite hilarious at the time. But now she got an uncomfortable sensation in her chest whenever she thought about the things she'd done. Undeniably mean things.

Chloe always told herself it had been for self-protection. A way of nipping things in the bud before they bloomed into something that might hurt Chloe instead of her victim. A way of turning the attention from one poor scholarship girl on to another. You had to get in there first, didn't you? To make sure those awful things didn't happen to you.

After all, when Chloe first joined West Cliff, she'd endured her fair share of being bullied by Abigail and her clique. But, unlike Laura, Chloe had eventually stood up for herself. Had toughened up. It helped that Harriet and Jas had taken Chloe under their wing. They'd had her back. Laura didn't really have any friends, but that wasn't Chloe's fault. She couldn't be expected to look out for everyone else. Not when she had her own battles to fight. And, anyway, Laura had all that talent. Had won all those medals. What did she have to feel sad about?

When Chris told her that he'd stumbled across Laura snogging another girl in the gym cupboard, Chloe was excited at the possibilities this yielded. She made him go back and take a photo of them with his smartphone. It was annoying that he hadn't managed to ID the other girl. 'She had brown hair,' Chris had said. 'Brown hair?' *Chloe replied, rolling her eyes. 'Well, that narrows it down.' She should've gone with him to take the photo, but she'd had to run to catch the bus. And the photo itself didn't give any clues as the other girl's face was partly turned away and in shadow.*

At least Laura hadn't spotted Chris at the time. That was the main thing. No, she was too busy getting her rocks off with her girlfriend.

Harriet and Jasmine were usually Chloe's partners in crime, but she didn't tell them about Laura's kiss. She'd planned on revealing her part in it once the excitement had died down and she was certain she wouldn't get into any trouble. Because although she liked her friends, she didn't exactly trust them to keep quiet about such a juicy piece of gossip. And it had to be a surprise – that was the whole point.

Chloe couldn't wait to see the looks on their faces when she owned up to being the mastermind. But then Laura went and did what she did – drowned herself in the school swimming pool, of all places. There was no way Chloe was telling anyone about her part in it after that. So, yeah, Chloe got a shock. Felt pretty sick for a while afterwards. But how was she supposed to know Laura would do something so unbelievably drastic? It was only supposed to be a bit of a laugh. Laura Rudd was obviously destined for great things, so Chloe had just wanted to keep her grounded. Give her a bit of humility before her rise to stardom.

She made Chris swear not to tell anyone that she was involved. He agreed, but she didn't fully trust him to keep his mouth shut. So she warned him that if he mentioned her name in connection with any of it, she'd go straight to his father and tell him about all the shit he got up to at school. That pissed him right off. Told her she was a sneaky bitch. They'd had a massive argument. But she's pretty sure he'll keep his mouth shut now. It was no skin off his nose anyway. He hadn't got into any trouble over it.

Chris actually forgave her for blackmailing him pretty quickly. Even wanted to get back with her. But Chloe has had just about enough of West Cliff School now, and all the people in it. She can't wait to put the whole horrible incident behind her and move on with her life. The only thing is that since it happened, she can't seem to stop crying. She can't stop seeing Laura's face on that screen, remembering her reaction in the hall. Picturing what she must have looked like in the pool – afterwards. All those upsetting images keep shuttling through Chloe's brain on a loop.

And the sad thing is, Chloe isn't sure she's going to be able to continue swimming. Not now. Because even the smell of chlorine makes her gag, makes her see Laura's sad, humiliated face in her mind, which sets off that never-ending loop of images.

It really is too bad.

Chapter Thirty-Nine

CHLOE

I wait in the lobby for Chris to show me up to his office. Too antsy to sit patiently in any of the plush chairs, I pace outside the bank of lifts, mulling over exactly what I'm going to say when I see him. I wanted to wear something to give me confidence today. Something smart and neutral that doesn't send any mixed messages. I think this outfit does the job – a camel-coloured trouser suit with a black shell top and black boots, my newly highlighted hair held back off my face with a tortoiseshell comb. Professional. No nonsense.

When I first contacted Chris to arrange this meeting, he suggested I came to his house, but I thought it more sensible to meet at his place of work rather than the intimate setting of his home, where there was the unwelcome possibility of things becoming more personal.

Meeting with Chris isn't something I'm looking forward to, but I have to do something about these anonymous emails. Chris is the only person who knows my secret. The only person who has the power to destroy my life. So I have to confront him. I have to put an end to his harassment once and for all.

The middle lift pings and slides open. I tense, bracing myself. The last time we saw one another was last year at the reunion. I didn't think I would be the one asking to meet up again, but I don't exactly have much choice in the matter. Not if I want to put this situation to rest.

A woman with shiny brown hair steps out of the lift. 'Chloe Flynn?' she asks.

I frown and nod.

'Nice to meet you.' She holds out a hand, which I shake unenthusiastically. 'I'm Melanie, Chris's assistant.'

'Hi.'

She gestures to the lift and I step in. It's annoying that Chris didn't come down to meet me himself. He had to send this *Melanie* down instead. He's obviously too big and important to greet me personally. Is it some kind of power game he's playing? Trying to wrongfoot me from the start?

Melanie presses a button. A second later, the door closes and the lift starts to ascend. It's just too bad that Chris knows what he knows – the fact that I was behind the photo of Laura, and now there's the whole Dean-trying-to-kill-him evening. I wonder if Chris has heard that Dean and I are engaged. Is he trying to hold my past over my head as some kind of weapon? He could end my happiness with a simple word in Dean's ear. I would deny it, but the seed would have been planted. Dean would never fully trust me again.

Thankfully, I have something I can threaten Chris with. Something that will keep him in line. I hope. But you never really know with Chris.

I realise Melanie has been speaking and is waiting for a reply, a friendly smile on her face.

'Sorry, I was miles away,' I say, just as the lift door opens, saving me from having to make small talk. I can't give my attention to anything other than the meeting ahead of me.

Melanie takes the hint and stays silent as I follow her along a wide corridor that's been done out in an Art Deco style to complement the building. She knocks on the door at the end and opens it, ushering me inside. She doesn't follow me into the room, and closes the door behind her with a loud click.

Chris's office is masculine and luxurious, light and spacious, with far-ranging views over the town. He's sitting behind a huge desk, watching me as I walk in. He makes no attempt to greet me, just follows my progress with his eyes, a lazy smile forming on his lips. Right now, I wish I'd gone to a different school and never met Chris Tamber. I wish he would just disappear from my life.

'Thanks for seeing me,' I say.

He gestures to one of the chairs in front of his desk. I don't want to sit, but I do, perching on the edge of the seat, glancing over his desk at the plans spread out across its surface. At his shiny MacBook and latest iPhone. At a Montblanc pen resting atop a sheaf of papers. I can't help being awed by this privileged world he inhabits. He owns this whole building and more besides. His main home these days is a multimillion-pound property set behind security gates. He's used to people falling at his feet and doing as he says. He wouldn't let anyone else talk to him the way I've done. But somehow he lets me get away with it. And I don't think it's just because of my attempt to blackmail him. He still holds a soft spot for me, for whatever reason. Although that hasn't stopped him from trying to intimidate me with his horrible emails.

'So,' he says, leaning back in his chair and interlocking his fingers. 'I hear you and Bradley got engaged . . .'

So he does know. But I'm not here to talk about my relationship with Dean, so I ignore his statement and get straight to the point. 'Have you been sending me anonymous emails?' I ask.

His eyebrows quirk together. 'Have I *what*?'

'I've been receiving threatening emails from someone. And they read like they're from you.'

'I'm hurt you would even think that, Chloe.' His eyes dance with amusement. 'What do these emails say?'

'The first ones warned me to stay away from the reunion.'

'I wish they'd sent one to me,' he replies earnestly. 'Would have saved me a lot of hassle. I've got a wicked scar on my arm from that night. Want to see?' He sits upright and starts removing his suit jacket.

'No, thanks.' I hold out my hand to stop him.

He shrugs and stops, leaning back into his chair again. 'Suit yourself. But it's quite impressive. Anyway, these emails . . . they didn't want you going to the reunion? But you went anyway. So why would you think I sent them? I was happy you came – to start with, anyway. By the end, not so much.'

'They're obviously from you. They say things like *Your secret isn't safe with me* and *What would Dean think if he knew what you did?* After the first few, I stopped reading them, but I had a quick scan of the latest ones and they're nasty. Telling me I'm a bitch and that I don't . . .' My throat tightens. 'That I don't deserve to live. Your usual threatening email scenario.' I'm aiming for a light-hearted tone, but my voice sounds strangled.

'Jesus, Chlo.' Chris frowns. 'That's not good. Have you reported them to the police? And why the hell would you think they're from me? We have our . . . *issues*. But you know I'd never do anything like that to you.'

'Do I though? You're the only one who knew I was anything to do with that photo, so who else could it have been?' I examine his features, trying to see behind the handsome facade, trying to work out if he's genuine. 'After what I said to you at the pool, you could've got angry afterwards and wanted to scare me. To pay me back.'

That night, when Dean threatened to kill Chris for his part in Laura's suicide, I worried that Chris was going to land me in it. That he was going to tell Dean that the whole projector prank had been my idea. So I lowered myself into the pool and swam over to Chris.

I made him promise not to report Dean to the police if he gave up the knife and allowed Chris to leave. I then whispered in his ear that if he so much as mentioned my name in connection with Laura, I would lie to his soon-to-be ex-wife, and say that Chris and I had an affair while they were still together. Which would lead to his wife getting a hell of a lot more in the divorce settlement. Money always talks with people like Chris.

He'd been furious with me at the time, but he knew me well enough to realise I wasn't bluffing. Dangling this threat over Chris's head is the only thing making me less nervous around him. Now that he owes me some respect, he won't be able to get away with the kind of stunt he pulled at the reunion – like harassing me, or forcing his attentions on me. He knows I won't take that shit from him any longer. Maybe the anonymous emails were the only way he could get his revenge.

'Of course I was angry with you,' Chris snaps, getting to his feet and turning to gaze out of the floor-to-ceiling window. 'You tried to blackmail me with a lie.' He turns back to glare at me. 'At least if you're going to blackmail me, let it be with something we've actually done. An affair with you would have been worth paying my ex-wife for. But an imaginary affair? Not so much.'

'So you're denying you sent those emails?' I ask, staring at his face for any hint of the truth.

'Anonymous emails aren't my style, Chlo. I'm far too busy for all that childish shit.'

I exhale, wondering if I can believe him. If he is the one behind them, did I really think he would admit it? 'I'll take them to the police,' I say. 'Get them to find out who they're from. So if it is you, you may as well admit it now.'

He tuts away my accusation. 'You *should* take them to the police,' he replies. 'Why haven't you done that already? Do you think this person's dangerous? I can get someone to investigate, if you like? I bet my guy could discover who it is quicker than the cops ever could.'

I shake my head, not wanting to get tangled up in anything else with Chris. If it is him, he's not about to admit it. I've reached a dead end here.

His dark eyes soften for a moment. 'Don't you miss us, Chlo? You and I, we're the same. We like fun and passion and thrills. Dean Bradley . . . he's a boring nobody. A loser. You'll get tired of him, Chlo. You know you will.'

I don't dignify Chris's smug prediction with a response. Dean and I are perfect together. We click. He's a good man. I've told myself that marrying Dean will be different to my previous marriage. Better. But is that really true?

I try to push out the unwelcome memories of how good Ben and I were when we first met. He was a kind and attentive husband. He adored me. But I became irritated with his fawning. With his need to please me all the time. So I pushed him away. I had affairs. I wasn't very nice. No. I can admit to myself that, by the end, I was a pretty horrible wife. He eventually grew a backbone and filed for a divorce. I shouldn't have been shocked by that. But I was. It actually made me respect him more. Gave me a twinge of regret that we were over. I had honestly thought Ben would stick by me through thick and thin. But it seemed I had pushed him too far. I think – no, I *know* – that he was a little scared of me by the end.

There was no repairing our marriage, but it still stung when he fell for perfect Wendi so quickly. When they created their little family together. It made me think about my father, and how he'd left my mother to start his new family. It made me wonder if there was something wrong with me and Mum that made us genetically unlovable. But surely I'm nothing like my mother! No. Ben simply wasn't the right man for me. It was obvious. Especially when I missed our friendship circle more than I missed *him*.

My relationship with Dean is different. Stronger. I'm older and wiser now. I know what I stand to lose so I'm not going to mess it up. I've learnt my lesson. I'm not like that anymore. I will never take Dean for granted. He's my second chance at life. This is an opportunity to do things right this time. A new place, a new man, a new start. And Dean is nothing like Ben. Dean is tough, no nonsense. He knows what he wants and he goes for it.

Of course, I feel huge remorse for what happened with Dean's sister, but the past is in the past, and I can't undo it, no matter how hard I wish I could. When I discovered that the man I'd fallen for was Dean Bradley rather than Nathan Blake, well, it was a terrible shock. I would never have gone anywhere near him at the reunion if I'd known who he really was. But by the time he came clean about his identity, I was already smitten. He can't ever know about my role in those events with his sister. I'll do anything to keep my secret hidden. It makes me very uneasy that Chris knows the truth. Very uneasy indeed.

For his part, Dean was stricken about lying to me at the reunion, about keeping his identity hidden from me, but he hadn't expected to fall in love. I tried to put him off me at first, of course I did. No matter how much I wanted to be with him, it didn't feel right to be with this man, in light of who he was. In light of my tangled history with his sister. But he kept up his pursuit of me. He was relentless, and I wasn't strong enough to keep turning him down. The truth is, I wanted to be with him. Was head over heels for the man.

Is it really so wrong to want to be with the man I love? Especially as he loves me back just as hard. To have pushed him away would have made us both miserable, and where's the sense in that? Do I wish he had been Nathan Blake rather than Dean Bradley? Of course. That would have made everything so much simpler. But I don't even know who the real Nathan is. He moved away years ago, and no one from around here is in touch with him anymore. Nathan was a fantasy, nothing more.

'I should go,' I say, realising this was a wasted journey. Chris was never going to admit to anything. I'll just have to hope that if it was him, he'll stop now that I've confronted him about it. Now that I've threatened to go to the police.

'When you get bored of Bradley, come and find me,' Chris says. He pauses. 'You're not going to live in his family house, though, surely?'

'My living arrangements are nothing to do with—'

Chris chokes out a disbelieving laugh. 'You are? The house where he and Laura grew up? That's a bit sick, even for you, Chlo.'

I clench my fists at my sides and try not to show how rattled I am by his observations. 'How do you know where Dean lives?' I snap.

'I made it my business to know everything about Bradley after he came here shouting his mouth off. But, Chlo, tell me you're not going to be moving into that house with him. How can you do it?'

I'll admit to myself that it made me a bit queasy, knowing we'd be moving into Dean's family home. I'd tried to dissuade him at first. Said that it might be better if we bought somewhere new together. A fresh start and all that. But he was adamant that he wanted to renovate his mother's house. He said we wouldn't recognise it when it was done. That we would pretty much gut the place and make it our own. Create new, happy memories.

I ended up agreeing. It will be fine, once we've erased all traces of her. Going into Laura's old bedroom is the worst but, aside from that, the main things creeping me out are the framed photos of her that sit in the lounge, and the ones that range all the way up the staircase wall, documenting almost every year of her life. Laura's haunted eyes seem to follow me whenever I walk past. Once we finally start decorating, I'll somehow arrange for them to be housed somewhere less conspicuous. Perhaps I'll create a photo wall in whichever room becomes Dean's office and move them all in there. Somewhere discreet where I never have to look at them.

'It's just a house, Chris.' I shrug, unclenching my fists, not wanting him to see how rattled I am.

'If you say so.'

I scowl at him.

'Well,' he says, coming around the desk and sitting in the chair next to me. 'Sorry I couldn't help with the email mystery.'

He's far too close for comfort so I get up and head over to the polished walnut sideboard, examining the drinks and picking up a heavy crystal tumbler.

'Bit early, even for you, isn't it, Chlo?'

I set the glass back on the tray with a clunk and turn to face him. 'If it wasn't you who sent the emails, I just need to check that you didn't tell anyone else about . . . you know, the thing with Laura being my idea?'

Chris doesn't reply straight away. He sniffs and cuts eye contact.

I glare at him in disbelief. '*Chris!* Who did you tell? Not your wife!'

'Sorry, can't say. But they won't let it slip. I made them promise. Believe me, they're very trustworthy.'

'You're such an idiot!' I stride over to where he's sitting and lean down so I'm millimetres from his face, the scent of his aftershave making me dizzy for a second before I pull myself together again and grit my teeth.

'Who. Did. You. Tell?'

His face blanches at my cold fury. But I'm not leaving this office until I get a name out of him.

Chapter Forty

CHLOE

The doorbell rings, a harsh, almost rattling sound that makes me jump. I leave the kitchen and check my face in the hall mirror before pulling open the front door.

'Come in!' I cry with a welcoming smile and then frown at the weather out there. 'Ugh, what a foul night.'

'It really is filthy,' she replies, shaking out her umbrella and leaving it to drain in the porch before stepping into the hallway. 'The walk over was treacherous. The trees are all swaying and creaking like something out of a horror movie.' She laughs. 'Thought I was going to get hit by a falling branch and end up on the local news.'

'You walked over from your place in this?'

'Only took ten minutes. Seemed like a good idea at the time.' Harriet looks me up and down and leans in for a hug. 'Feels like I haven't seen you for ages.'

'Sorry, I know. Everything's been so manic, what with sorting out my Bath flat and then the move down here, trying to bond with Ellis . . .' I grimace.

'Is it still not going well with him?'

I waggle my hand back and forth. 'Let's just say it could be better. He's an absolute sweetie, of course he is, but it's going to take a while to win him over. Thankfully, things with his dad are still amazing.' I grin and put a hand to my heart. 'Here, let me take your coat.' I hang her dripping parka on the banister and she peels off her hat and gloves as we smile at one another. 'It's so nice of you to do this,' I add.

'It's my pleasure,' Harriet says, gazing around, taking in the narrow hall with its nineties wallpaper and worn beige carpet. 'What's life all about if we can't help one another out?'

'Well, I appreciate it. And you can definitely invoice us for your time.'

She waves away my offer with her free hand.

Dean is out with mates this evening and won't be back till late, and Ellis is having a sleepover with his best friends, Isla and Grace. He was so excited about it he could barely sit still all day. So it's just me and Harriet here – a chance for us to catch up on what's been happening, and for her to give me some ideas for the new extension in her capacity as an interior designer.

'Is it too early for wine?' I offer. 'Or would you prefer a cuppa?'

'Definitely wine,' she replies with a grin, following me through to the kitchen. 'Why do you think I left the car at home?'

'So you were prepared to risk being hit by falling branches just to have a glass of wine?' I ask.

'Yep, totally a risk worth taking.'

I laugh and reach into the fridge for an opened bottle of Sauvignon Blanc. 'Well, I hope this label doesn't disappoint.'

'I'm sure it will be fine.' She takes in the old-fashioned kitchen with its dated wooden cabinets and chipped laminate worktops. 'So this is the area that's going to be extended?'

I straighten up and gesture around the room. 'Yes, like I said, we're knocking the kitchen and dining room through and adding on a four-metre extension out the back.'

'Nice,' she replies, nodding and glancing around. 'The dining room's through there?' she asks, pointing to the far wall.

'Yes.' I reach up to one of the cabinets for a glass and pour out a generous measure of wine. 'That wall will be coming down.'

'And what's the overall width of the space going to be?'

'Eight metres. So the whole kitchen-dining-living area will be eight by seven. And then there's the separate living room at the front to decorate too.' I'm so excited at the prospect of making this into our dream home, I can barely keep the grin from my face.

'Are you wanting a modern feel, or traditional?' Harriet asks. 'It's a nice 1930s home, so you could do something with a Deco twist.'

I think about Chris's 1930s office block and shake my head, not wanting anything that reminds me of him. 'Dean wants ultra-modern, but I'd like to keep the period features. So maybe—'

'Ooh, okay, well, how about you go super contemporary in here, and then keep the front lounge as a cosy traditional snug?'

'That sounds good,' I reply brightly, while thinking it sounds a bit vague. 'Depends what you mean by "super contemporary" . . .'

'Well, there are a few ways you could go. How about I get some ideas down and send them over to you?'

'That would be wonderful, if you're sure you don't mind?'

'I'd love to. Whatever you decide on, I'm sure it's going to be a stunning space.'

'I know, right? The foundation's being poured tomorrow, so it'll soon be all systems go.'

'You not having any wine?' she asks with a frown. 'Not pregnant, are you?'

'No, no, nothing like that. No, I'd love to have a drink, but, like I said, I'm getting the train up to Bristol tonight for this two-day life-coaching course and I'm driving to the station. Plus I want to keep a clear head.'

'Oh, that's right, you did say. What time do you need to get going? Don't worry, I won't keep you.'

'Not for at least another half-hour. The actual course doesn't start until tomorrow, but there's a dinner at the hotel later.' I pour myself a glass of water and think about how lucky I am to be able to retrain for a career that actually interests me. I haven't been this fired up about anything since my swimming days. Of course, I haven't done the course yet, so I can't be absolutely sure it's for me. But I'm excited to give it a go.

'Life coaching, eh?' Harriet raises an eyebrow.

'Yeah. I want a more interesting job,' I reply. 'Something that's flexible, where I can maybe work from home. Plus,' I add with a smile, 'I've made so many screw-ups in my life that, as a life coach, I'd be helping people from a place of experience.'

'Ha! Well, you can book me in for a session once you're qualified,' Harriet says. 'We could all do with a little life coaching.'

'Sure, but you don't seem to need it,' I reply. 'I've never met anyone who's got their shit together more than you, Harrie.'

'Nice of you to say, but things aren't always what they look like on the outside.'

'Oh?' I cock my head, wondering if she'll elaborate.

She smiles and shakes her head, taking a sip of her drink, making it clear that she doesn't want to talk about it.

But her silence doesn't fool me. I know what she's been up to.

Chapter Forty-One

CHLOE

Harriet and I move next door into the chilly dining room, where she outlines one of her visions for the new space and I make impressed noises. But I'm not really listening anymore. I keep glancing at her, wondering how she can be acting so normally around me when she's been keeping all these secrets. Although I suppose I've been doing exactly the same. Still, I'd thought she was my friend. I'd been looking forward to years more friendship with her and Jas. The three of us sharing our hopes and dreams, having kids, family life, maybe holidays together. I guess that's off the cards now.

When I went to visit him in his office last week, Chris told me that he'd had a fling with Harriet before the reunion. That snippet of information had shocked me quite a lot. I couldn't picture the two of them together. They don't seem like each other's type. I guess Chris must be the mystery man Harriet was so secretive about. Perhaps she was worried I'd be angry that she'd slept with my ex. She needn't have worried on that score. Chris and I were over years ago.

Chris said he hadn't really been that interested in her, but she'd thrown herself at him on a night out, right when he was newly separated from his wife, Polly. He told me he hadn't been thinking straight at the time, and anyway, who was he to turn down a free shag?

With the reunion coming up, the two of them had got talking about school and the prom, and Harriet asked him if he regretted posting up that picture of Laura. The stupid idiot told her that the photo was my idea. I couldn't believe Chris had betrayed my trust like that. I'd told him that he'd better not tell anyone else. He shrugged an apology, but didn't seem to think it was a big deal.

I then realised that it must have been Harriet who'd been sending me the emails. That she was messing with me for some reason. That she possibly had a screw loose. Maybe she was upset when I ended our friendship all those years ago. Maybe she was jealous of me. Maybe she really was in love with Chris and didn't like the fact that he still had a thing for me. But, whatever the reason, I needed to find out. I couldn't have her knowing my secret and potentially blabbing to Dean. This whole situation was getting out of control. Running away from me. It made me sick to think of the potential fallout.

Chris told me I was blowing things out of proportion. But I'd replied that if Harriet knew I was the one behind the photo, then why hadn't she just asked me about it, instead of keeping it secret? She must have had some ulterior motive for not telling me she knew. Chris shook his head and told me the reason she hadn't said anything was that he'd sworn her to secrecy. *Not everyone is as devious as you, Chlo*, he'd said with his usual knowing smirk.

But I can't risk Harriet telling Dean what she knows. She could ruin my life just as it's truly beginning.

'Changing the subject slightly, but there's something I've been meaning to show you,' I say to Harriet as she's explaining the different options of Velux windows, skylights or roof lights.

'Oh?' She breaks off and gives me a quizzical look.

I take out my phone – a brand-new water-resistant iPhone that I bought after Abigail's drunken phone attack – and open up my messages. I show Harriet the horrible emails I've been receiving and watch her reaction.

'These are awful!' she says, looking at me in horror, and placing a hand on my arm. 'Do you know who sent them?'

'No idea. They started up just before the reunion, warning me not to come. But whoever it is, they never stopped sending them. I thought they might be from Abigail Matthews, but . . .' I shrug.

'What are you going to do?' Harriet asks, her eyes full of concern. 'Have you been to the police?'

'Not yet. I'm thinking about it though. See if they're able to trace whoever's responsible. I'm hoping the police will take it seriously, what with there being death threats and everything.' I scrutinise Harriet's face for a reaction, but she just nods and says that's probably the best thing to do.

Maybe I'm barking up the wrong tree, and it *wasn't* Harriet who sent them . . . but who else would it be? No. I'm certain it's her. She's probably just a really good actor. I can't let her innocent expression fool me.

'I'm gasping for a ciggie,' she says. 'Reading those messages has made me feel quite out of sorts.' She gives a shiver. 'I can't imagine how you must be feeling. They're horrible.'

'I usually let them go straight into my spam folder without reading them,' I reply. 'They're not very nice, but I just keep telling myself that whoever sent them is a coward. Spineless. Pretty sick, actually. Think I'll join you for a smoke,' I add, hoping a cigarette might help to calm my booming heart. 'It's a bit muddy out the back though.'

'I don't mind that,' Harriet replies. 'I'm used to traipsing round building sites in my line of work.'

We grab our coats, hats and gloves, and Harriet pulls a pack of Marlboro and a lighter from her bag. I leave my phone on the counter and we slip out through the back door, sheltering under the scaffolding next to the metre-and-a-half pit that's now ready for the foundations to be poured. Dean made the trench deeper than it needs to be as the soil is quite sandy around here, so he wants to ensure the extension will be rock solid.

As Harriet lights both cigarettes and passes one to me, I open my mouth and start speaking the words that have been on the tip of my tongue ever since she arrived.

'I know it was you who sent the emails,' I say bluntly, before taking a drag of my cigarette.

'*What?*' She looks outraged for a moment, until I give her a knowing glare and her shoulders drop. 'Fine, busted, it was me,' she says, sounding only mildly annoyed.

'*Harriet!* How *could* you?' I hadn't been entirely certain. I'd actually hoped I was wrong. But now that she's admitted it, I feel so disappointed. Let down. Sick. 'I honestly thought you were my friend. Is it because you're in love with Chris? Because you know I only have eyes for Dean . . .'

She tuts and exhales, smoke curling around her head like a hydra. 'In love with Chris? Hardly. The man's a self-obsessed prick.'

'So when you told me and Jas you were interested in someone, it wasn't Chris you were interested in?'

'No. I only said that to stop you both trying to set me up with some godawful person from school.'

'So then, *why*?' I ask.

'Because Chris told me it was your idea to post that photo of Laura,' she says curtly. 'Outing her in front of the whole school.'

I shake my head regretfully. 'I know it was a terrible thing to have done, but I was a stupid kid who thought it would be funny. Anyway,' I add, narrowing my eyes at her, 'I seem to remember you thought it was hilarious at the time, so I'm not sure why you're getting on your high horse about it.'

'Nothing funny about bullying someone so badly that they kill themselves,' she replies tersely.

I swallow and grit my teeth, dropping my cigarette into the deep hole, watching as the spark glows orange and then dies. 'It wasn't like that,' I say, my protest feeling weak to my ears.

'It was exactly like that.' Harriet's glare doesn't leave my face. 'I know we weren't exactly the sweetest teenagers in the world, Chloe, but what you did . . . you took things to a whole other level. There was nothing about what you did that was acceptable.'

'And sending me threatening messages *is*?' I retort.

'It's what you deserve, Chloe. You get off on making people's lives miserable. Thought you could do with a taste of your own medicine.'

'We were kids!' I cry. 'I was a stupid teenager. You know I'm not like that anymore.'

'Being young doesn't excuse you. There are millions of teenagers in the world. You think they all get off on torturing people?'

'Are you going to tell Dean?' I ask, knowing that whatever she says, it won't change my mind. I know what I have to do.

Harriet takes a step closer so she's standing right at the edge of the foundation pit. She gazes steadily at me as the rain drips off the scaffolding on to her cheek. She takes a last drag on her cigarette and grinds it out on the wet scaffold pole, placing the butt in her pocket. 'You should tell Dean yourself,' she replies. 'You don't want to go into marriage with that kind of secret hanging over your head. How can you even think about being with him after what you did to his sister?'

I shudder at the thought of Dean's expression if he ever found out. At all the hurt and anger that would be directed towards me. 'It would break his heart,' I say defensively.

'It would break up your relationship, you mean,' she replies with a sneer.

Harriet's right. I think back to how Dean wanted to hurt Chris when he thought he was solely responsible for Laura's death. I remember the rage in Dean's eyes. With me, it would be a thousand times worse. He would see it as a betrayal of the lowest kind.

A helpless, desperate, panicky feeling rolls through me. I can't risk Dean ever looking at me with that same expression. I need to clarify things with Harriet tonight. Get this sorted once and for all. 'So, I guess this means that if I don't tell him, you will,' I reply flatly. 'I was hoping you might have valued our friendship a bit more than that. I was hoping you might have cut me some slack, knowing we were just kids back then. We were good friends. Best friends. Surely that counts for something.'

She stays silent, watching my eyes until I blink and look away.

'Have you told Jasmine about all this?' I ask, dreading the answer.

Harriet shakes her head. 'No. This is between you and me. No need to involve anyone else.'

I breathe a sigh of relief, thanking God for small mercies. Once this is done, I can move on with my life.

'Chloe . . .' Harriet says, staring directly at me with a strange expression on her face. 'Didn't you ever wonder who the other girl in the photo was?'

'Of course I wondered,' I reply, shaking my head. 'Everyone wondered. But Chris didn't get a look at her. Her back was to the camera. He couldn't . . . *Oh.*' My breath hitches as Harriet continues to gaze at me and realisation dawns.

'*You.*' I exhale. 'You and Laura.'

Chapter Forty-Two

CHLOE

Harriet's eyes glisten as she confirms what I've just realised – that Laura and Harriet were the two girls kissing in the gym cupboard that day.

'Laura was my first love,' Harriet says, blinking back her emotion. 'My only love really. And she died thinking that I betrayed her. Which of course I didn't, not in the way she thinks. But . . .' She takes a breath. 'But I did betray her, in a way, because I was too scared to go over to her that night at the prom. To let her know that I still loved her. Instead, I was gutless, laughing with you all, pretending the whole thing was hilarious, when inside . . . I wanted to die. Knowing how much it was hurting her. Knowing that she might think I'd set her up. Thinking that I didn't really love her at all. When I did.'

A cold sensation grips the back of my neck. Harriet doesn't just know what Chris and I did; she has skin in the game. This is personal to her. There's nothing I can say. She'll never forgive me. She'll never let this go.

Harriet stares out into the gloomy garden as the rain thickens and swirls. A moment passes before she continues talking. 'After Laura left the prom, I was too nervous to get in touch with her straightaway. I didn't know how to explain my behaviour. I hadn't been brave enough to out myself in front of everyone that night, but I was terrified that she might condemn me for not standing up to you all. For not telling you how disgusting you all were. But, most of all, I was scared of seeing the hurt on her face. I was basically a coward. I left it too late to apologise, to beg her forgiveness, and I've regretted it ever since.'

I listen to Harriet continue to pour her heart out, telling me how kind and sweet and funny Laura was. How genuine and talented and driven. And while of course I'm sympathetic to her, I'm only half listening, still reeling from Harriet's revelation. I realise that, however sad her story is, I'm still as determined as ever to put an end to this, once and for all. I can't let sentimentality ruin my happiness with Dean. I just can't. The stakes are too high. I've waited too long for my life to begin properly.

'You and Chris as good as killed Laura,' she says through gritted teeth. 'Outing her in front of everyone like that was beyond vile. No one really believed her death was an accident. You drove her to suicide and you ruined my chance at happiness with the person I loved.'

I open my mouth to apologise, to lure Harriet into a false sense of security while I act. My heart is pounding wildly. I'll never get as good a chance as now. All I need to do is slip this knife out of my pocket, stick her with it and give her a good, hard shove into the—

A sharp pain cracks across my head. I blink as everything blurs. When I open my eyes, I see Harriet standing with a brick in her hand, one corner of it covered in blood. I put a hand to the side of my head as she leans forward and pushes my upper body hard.

I'm bleeding! I'm falling! This isn't right. This isn't what I planned. I was about to do something important, but I can't quite remember . . .

Harriet is still talking, her words weaving in and out of my hearing as I land with an awkward, painful thud.

'I wasn't brave enough to stick up for Laura that night at the prom,' she says, her voice filled with pain and anger. 'I pretended not to know the girl she was kissing. I mocked her. Mocked myself. But only because I was scared of you. Of Chris. You terrorised everyone, Chloe. I never realised that you and the swim team were such bitches to Laura. She only told me about it towards the end. I was glad you never wanted to keep in touch after school because I don't think I could have looked at you back then without spitting in your face. It's taken all my acting skills to pretend to like you, these past few months. The only thing that kept me going was knowing I'd make you suffer eventually. That I would find a way to make you pay. Why should you get your happily ever after when you've ruined everyone else's?'

As I lie face up in the dirt, I blink the rain from my lashes to see Harriet peering down at me, a pale looming figure. She looks so close and yet so far away. My body feels numb and soft as I lie in our newly dug foundations. The epicentre of the pain in my head is sharp, but the rest feels warm and liquid, like boiling water being poured over my skull.

'I've been living in denial for fifteen years,' Harriet continues, her voice drilling into my brain. 'I've been frozen in time. Knowing that Chris did this horrible thing, but unable to act. Unable to get revenge. Too scared to do anything. So I buried it all. Pretended it never happened.

'But then the invitation to the reunion arrived in my inbox, and it unlocked something inside me, brought all my emotions rushing to the surface. It got me thinking about Chris Tamber and how he'd ended a life and stolen my happiness. I suddenly knew what I had to do to fix things. I realised that Chris had to pay for what he'd done. It was the only way I'd be able to get any peace.

The only way I could move on with my life. I've been emotionally stuck for fifteen years.' Harriet has a shovel in her hand and is dumping earth on top of my body. I try to speak. To plead with her, but my whole body is numb, paralysed. All I can do is blink . . . and listen . . . to the wind and the rain and to Harriet's incessant whining explanation.

'So I pretended to fancy Chris,' she continues, shovelling earth on to my legs. 'After I got the reunion invite, I virtually threw myself at him. I slept with him, pretended he was great in bed – he wasn't. Finally got him to open up about Laura. Surprisingly, he was remorseful.' Harriet chokes out a bitter laugh.

'I was going to kill him there and then in his bed, but he let slip something about how he never should have let *you* talk him into it. When he mentioned your name and said that you were the one behind the whole thing, I thought I was going to lose it. I don't know how I kept my shit together. But I did. I abandoned my plan to kill Chris and decided there and then what I should do instead.' Harriet leans on the shovel for a moment, catching her breath as the wind whips her hair around her face.

I wait for her to elaborate, although, of course, lying here, I already know the answer.

'I decided to reignite our friendship, kill you, and frame Chris for your murder,' she says. 'Simple. That way, you both pay for your cruelty and poor Dean won't fall under suspicion, because if you disappear, the partner is usually the first person the police will want to talk to.

'Those anonymous emails you received are traceable back to a burner phone that I used Chris's credit card to pay for online. I cloned his card the night I slept with him.' She resumes shovelling earth. I feel heavy clumps of it landing on my thighs and on my torso. Mud splashes on to my face. Into my mouth as I open it to try to speak again. Desperate now to make a plea, but still nothing comes out but a faint gurgling rasp. The mud is cold and wet and thick on my tongue. I don't have the strength to spit it out so it slides into my throat, sitting there, making me gag.

'No one will miss you for at least a couple of days,' Harriet explains matter-of-factly. 'By that time, you'll be dead and covered in concrete. Oh, that reminds me . . .' She disappears for a few moments. When she returns, she crouches and leans into the pit, holding something in front of my face. My phone. She uses facial recognition to unlock it. 'Perfect,' Harriet says, tapping at the screen with her gloved fingers. 'Special phone gloves,' she explains. 'I'm sending Chris an angry, upset text from you, explaining that Dean is out and you need Chris to come over to the house right now. Because, of course, he needs to be spotted at the scene of the crime on the night it happens. I'll make sure to leave the front door open so he can walk straight in.

'Pretty sure I've got everything covered,' Harriet continues. 'I'll park your car near the train station so Dean doesn't wonder why you didn't take it. I'll pay another visit to Chris this week. Leave some of your hair on his clothes, maybe some of this earth, too. I'll also plant some of Chris's hair and fibres from his clothes in your house and I've pressed some on to this brick,' she says, tossing it in after me. It scrapes my cheek, but I barely feel it. 'I'll leave other clues to link the two of you. But basically, it will be an unrequited love situation. He loved you, but you loved Dean, he couldn't stand to see the two of you happy, yada, yada, yada – you get the idea. You wanted to have things out with him tonight, but he got angry and things went too far and he killed you.'

The pain in my head still pulses, but my whole body is cold now. Icy. I need to move, to get myself out of this pit, to stop Harriet somehow. But my body won't obey me. I'm paralysed. I realise, with a stab of shock, that I'm actually dying. That Harriet is right – I won't get to live my happy-ever-after with Dean and Ellis.

I won't get to have more children or grandchildren. What will happen to my flat? To my mum? I want to tell Harriet that her killing me is not fair to Dean. That he'll miss me, he'll be heartbroken, but she seems to have thought of everything . . .

'Of course, poor Dean will be shocked by your death at first,' she says, her voice floating down as my life oozes into the sticky mud. 'But I'm sure he'll get over it pretty quickly once the whole sordid truth comes out about what you did to Laura. Once he realises you were the one who drove his sister to suicide. In fact, Dean will end up hating you. He'll probably want to congratulate Chris for finishing you off. Or maybe not. Chris wasn't exactly his favourite person. The main thing is that during the murder investigation I'll make sure Dean discovers what you did. That he'll realise exactly what sort of a person you are. Or *were,* should I say.'

Shovels of wet earth continue to rain down as she talks. 'Dean shouldn't have to grieve your death, or think of you as this good person he lost. He should know the truth. So that he can move on and eventually be happy with someone who deserves his love.' She stops shovelling for a moment, leans on the spade and gives a satisfied little laugh. 'It's a good thing your death won't upset Ellis too much. He never took to you in the first place. Kids are sharp – they can usually sniff out the rotten eggs.'

Harriet's words fade out as my thoughts turn inward. I was on the verge of having everything I'd ever wished for – a husband, a family, good friends, a new career, a wonderful fresh start. But now my mouth is filling with earth and my panicked thoughts are slowing. Dulling. Slipping into nothing.

I lock eyes with Harriet one last time – a piercing, pleading stare – until she dumps another shovelful of earth on my face and everything goes dark.

ACKNOWLEDGEMENTS

Huge thanks to Sammia Hamer, my wonderful editor. I've loved working with you on *The School Reunion*. Continued gratitude to my developmental editor – the superb Hannah Bond – for whipping this story into shape!! Thank you to Eoin Purcell, Rebecca Hills, Nicole Wagner and everyone else at Amazon Publishing who has helped bring this book into the world. I'm forever grateful for all your hard work and talent.

Thank you to Jenni Davis for doing a fantastic job on the copy-edits, and to Sarah Day for an excellent proofread.

Endless gratitude to author and police officer Sammy H. K. Smith for advising on the police procedure. As always, any mistakes and embellishments are my own.

Huge thanks to all at Brilliance for another incredible audiobook where you brought my story to life.

I'm so thankful to my beta readers Julie Carey and Terry Harden for always having the time and enthusiasm to comb through my books with such care. Thanks also to my readers – the bloggers, the reviewers, the sharers, recommenders and tweeters – too many to mention, plus I'm scared of accidentally leaving someone out. None of this would have been possible without you!

As always, huge gratitude to Neil, Charu, beautiful Siya, and John. And to all my friends and family for your constant love and support. Thank you times a million to Pete Boland, who is the most fantastic husband ever. To the Dowager Countess Jess, my fluffy and demanding writing companion. And finally, thank you to my children. You always stay kind, funny and upbeat, despite the obstacles you've already had to face. The world is a better place with you in it. I've said it many times before, but I'll say it again – you make me proud and grateful to be your mum.

A LETTER FROM THE AUTHOR

I just want to say a huge thank you for reading *The School Reunion*. I hope you enjoyed it. If you'd like to keep up to date with my latest releases, just sign up to my newsletter via my website and I'll let you know when I have a new novel coming out. Your email address will never be shared and you can unsubscribe at any time.

I love getting feedback on my books, so if you have a few moments, I'd be really grateful if you'd be kind enough to post a review online or tell your friends about it. A good review absolutely makes my day!

Shalini

ABOUT THE AUTHOR

Author photo © Shalini Boland 2022

Shalini Boland is the Amazon and *USA Today* bestselling author of eighteen psychological thrillers. To date, she's sold over two million copies of her books.

Shalini lives by the sea in Dorset, England, with her husband, two children and their increasingly demanding dog, Queen Jess. Before kids, she was signed to Universal Music Publishing as a singer/songwriter, but now she spends her days writing (in between restocking the fridge and dealing with endless baskets of laundry).

She is also the author of two bestselling sci-fi and fantasy series as well as a WWII evacuee adventure with a time-travel twist.

When she's not reading, writing or stomping along the beach, you can reach her via Facebook at www.facebook.com/ShaliniBolandAuthor, on Twitter @ShaliniBoland, on Instagram @shaboland, TikTok @shaliniboland or via her website: www.shaliniboland.co.uk.

Follow the Author on Amazon

If you enjoyed this book, follow Shalini Boland on Amazon to be notified when the author releases a new book!

To do this, please follow these instructions:

Desktop:

1) Search for the author's name on Amazon or in the Amazon App.
2) Click on the author's name to arrive on their Amazon page.
3) Click the 'Follow' button.

Mobile and Tablet:

1) Search for the author's name on Amazon or in the Amazon App.
2) Click on one of the author's books.
3) Click on the author's name to arrive on their Amazon page.
4) Click the 'Follow' button.

Kindle eReader and Kindle App:

If you enjoyed this book on a Kindle eReader or in the Kindle App, you will find the author 'Follow' button after the last page.